Rot
by Jenn

WILD THINGS

SHIFTERS UNBOUND

JENNIFER ASHLEY

Chapter One

Mason McNaughton jolted out of a sound sleep when several hundred pounds of enraged Feline landed on his chest and started to rip the hell out of him.

Mason rolled out from under the deadly claws, shifting as he went. He came up in his half-wolf form, grabbed the Feline around the waist and threw him into the wall. The wildcat bounced off and used the momentum to crash back into Mason.

They both went down, landing on the edge of the bed, which collapsed with a massive clatter. The wooden frame splintered, the mattress sliding off and pinning Mason with the Feline on top of him. Mason's Collar triggered, shocking and sparking pain into his neck, but if he stopped fighting, he'd die.

Mason's half-beast form gave him the strength to battle for his life. It also let him yell.

"Son of a bitch, get this fucking feral off me!"

He heard running in the hallway and then his oldest brother, Broderick, burst into the room with his usual energy. Broderick grabbed the snarling, spitting Feline and tried to yank him away from Mason.

The Feline turned around and went for Broderick, who was in human form and wearing nothing but a small pair of underwear. Broderick's skin reddened with blood as the Feline's claws raked his unprotected skin.

Mason launched himself off the floor, landing on the Feline and dragging him from Broderick. Broderick, swearing and bleeding, came back fighting.

"Aleck!" Broderick shouted at the Feline. *"Stop!"*

The Feline didn't even acknowledge his own name. He was far gone in the feral state, snarling and biting, his green cat eyes a crazed and burning red.

They'd have to kill the bastard this time for sure. What if he hadn't burst into Mason's room but Broderick and Joanna's, or Aunt Cora's?

Mason wrestled the Feline down, his wolf claws tearing through the cat's fur, drawing blood. Broderick was shifting, Mason saw out of the corner of his eye. The feral Aleck was a writhing ball of wildness, ready to gut everyone in the room, the house, maybe all of Shiftertown.

Mason knew they wouldn't be able to stop him short of breaking his neck. Aleck's mate was ready to drop a cub, and killing him would bring her terrible grief. But they had to stop him before he slaughtered the rest of the house.

Broderick became his full gray wolf and landed in the fray. He and Mason dodged giant cat paws and the snarling mouth, the wildcat's ears flat on his head. Aleck had no idea who they were—who *he* was. He was only following his instincts, killing the Lupines he thought were threats to his mate, no matter that Aleck was alive at all because of Mason and his brothers.

Aleck, unlike Broderick and Mason, didn't wear a shock Collar. Broderick's Collar was sparking as deeply as Mason's, slowing him down, while Aleck was free to surrender to the deadly violence that lurked inside every Shifter.

No more delays. Mason saw that thought flash through Broderick's eyes as well. Mason moved to grab the Feline in a headlock. He would break Aleck's neck and take the fall for it—Broderick couldn't do it because he was alpha and would need to calm down the rest of the family after Aleck was dead. As the youngest, Mason was expendable, at the bottom of this family's little pack.

The Feline slipped out of Mason's hold, turned around, and sank every one of his front claws into Mason's stomach, ripping it open. Mason's yell mixed with a howl as his full wolf took over. His reason faded as the crazed battle beast inside him rose, and he went for the kill.

Mason barely heard the noise just inside the doorway, but a second later, Broderick was tumbling him out of the way. There was a soft bang, a thunk, and the Feline let out a cat shriek that bored into Mason's brain and stayed there.

The Feline's scream died to a whimper. He collapsed in a tangle of limbs and tail, his green eyes half closing as his breathing wound down into that of peaceful sleep.

Mason dragged his head up. In the doorway stood Joanne, Broderick's mate, her hair sleep tousled, her nightshirt dragging down one shoulder. She peered over the barrel of a tranq rifle, eyeing Aleck to make sure he stayed asleep.

Broderick shifted back to his human form. His underwear had torn off in his change to wolf, and now he stood up, in the state Aunt Cora called butt-naked — the butt in question too much in Mason's view.

"Thank you, sweetheart," Broderick said breathlessly.

Joanne smiled back at Mason's brother, very much in love with the dirtbag. The little protrusion in her belly was the obvious symbol of that love.

Aunt Cora, in a hot pink bathrobe with bunnies on it, popped around Joanne and took in the scene. "Thank the Goddess," she said. "Mason, you all right? *Mason* …?"

Mason felt himself shifting back to human. He lay against the wall, unable to move, his stomach raked open and gushing blood.

"Don't worry," he tried to say, but it came out all slurred. "I'm f—" The rest of the word faded, as did the room, and Mason slid into oblivion.

***

The good thing about having a half-Shifter, half-Fae Lupine with healing powers in this Shiftertown was not only that she lived close by but also that she was gorgeous. Might be the painkillers she had given him talking, but Mason didn't mind looking his fill as Andrea Gray stitched up his wounds and sank her healing magic into him with the brush of her fingers.

So what if she was already mated to the Shiftertown's Guardian? Mason had no intention of touching the woman—she was a distant member of Mason's clan, in any case—but he could at least enjoy the beauty of her while she worked.

For some reason, though Aleck had attacked him, everyone was pissed off at *Mason*. Aleck, finally waking from his tranqued state, had been calm, his feral nature temporarily tucked away. He couldn't remember much, but he was pretty sure Mason had gone for him first, and Aleck had instinctively retaliated.

Mason, groggy from the painkillers, could only mumble in his defense. Nancy, Aleck's mate, had glared at Mason and asked why Mason couldn't accept that Aleck was ill and to leave him alone.

Goddess save me. Mason's room was a wreck, and there was no extra bedroom in this effing house for him to move into—no extra bed, period. He had to lie on the couch in the living room downstairs while Andrea sewed him up, which annoyed his three older brothers because they wanted to watch basketball.

Shifters had grown used to living in close quarters after being shoved into Shiftertowns, but this house was just getting stupid. Mason and his three brothers lived there with Aunt Cora, who kept them in line. Then Broderick had rescued Joanne's sister, Nancy, and had dragged home Aleck, her mate, a Feline pretty far gone into the feral state. Broderick had let them both live here so that *his* mate, Joanne, who also lived here now, would be happy.

Someone should have put Aleck out of his misery a long time ago, in Mason's opinion. But then Nancy and her unborn cub would be grief-stricken, Joanne would be upset that her sister was unhappy, and Broderick would become even harder to live with than he already was.

But what the hell were they going to do? Nancy would drop her cub any day, and Joanne was due in the fall. No one could predict what a feral Shifter would do to a tiny cub, even his own.

Ferals were Shifters who'd reverted into the wild things that lay at the core of every Shifter, the beast that reason deserted. The Shifter who started to slide into the feral state stopped bathing, forgot what forks were for, slept on the floor, and then just generally went foam-at-the-mouth crazy. Plus, ferals stank. The level of rank in this house had been steadily rising.

Most ferals either ran off into the wilderness to die of exposure, or they were killed by other Shifters to keep them from endangering the cubs. Aleck got to stay here and make their lives miserable while he hovered between sanity and the feral state. One day, though, they'd have to tranq him until he never woke up.

"Can't you do anything?" Mason asked Andrea as she sponged off his wound. "You're a healer. Fix him. Or at least make him smell better."

Andrea shook her head, dark hair moving in the spring breeze from the open windows. She was half Fae, which made her scent odd, but it was a hell of a lot better than feral Shifter. The draft blowing through the house didn't even make a dent in the stink from upstairs.

"I can heal wounds," Andrea said in her liquid voice. "Like yours." Light fingertips moved over Mason's stomach, the tingle of magic in them warm. "But Aleck is too far gone for me to reach, even if I knew how." Her brow furrowed in concern. "I'm not sure what we can do. Liam's called a meeting."

Liam, the Austin Shiftertown's leader, was a Feline, but in spite of that drawback, he wasn't such a bad guy, even Mason had to admit. Liam decided what was good for Shiftertown and what to do about problems like Aleck.

"Liam's called a meeting for when?" Mason asked. "I'm going."

"It's starting now, but you're staying here." Andrea gave him a stern look.

"No." Mason pushed her warm hands away and struggled to his feet. His belly was a mess of lines and stitches, but Shifters healed quickly, and all this pain would go away soon. Right?

"Mason ..." Andrea's grip on his arm was surprisingly strong. "Broderick ..."

"Sit your ass down, Mason." Broderick loomed up from the dining room where they'd dragged the television. The Spurs were playing to rave enthusiasm from their human—and Shifter—fans. "I'm heading to Liam's meeting to tell him all about what happened."

"*Aleck's* version of the story," Mason said. He grabbed his T-shirt and eased it over his hurt stomach then carefully buttoned and buckled his jeans. "He's a fekking liar if he says I attacked him. I was *asleep* when that ton of Feline landed on me."

"Not a liar," Broderick said, trying to sound reasonable. "Ferals don't always know what's going on."

"Which is why we have to do something about him." Mason's voice turned to a snarl. Broderick was his alpha, but Mason couldn't hold back his defiance. Mason knew Broderick wasn't happy with the Aleck situation either, but his word was law in this house ... well, as long as Aunt Cora and Joanne didn't argue with him.

Broderick's eyes narrowed. "Mason, I'm taking care of it. Get back on that couch and heal up. Andrea, tranq him or something."

Andrea shook her head and put her torturing needle back into her bag along with the medications she'd brought. "I'm not getting into a family fight, Broderick." She stood up and headed for the door without any apology.

"'Fraidy-cat," Mason called after her. The painkillers were making him a little woozy.

Andrea turned around and gave him a very wolf growl. "I'm mated to a Feline, and he's never afraid."

"No I meant ... Never mind." Mason grabbed a motorcycle boot and tried to jam it on his foot. He realized it was Broderick's, kicked it off, and fished under the coffee table for his own.

By the time Mason got his boots on and made it to the front porch, Broderick was beside him. "I said I have this," Broderick said, scowling.

"You're busy," Mason said, hanging on to the railing, the world spinning slightly. "You've got a mate and a cub on the way and people to boss around. *I'm* the one who nearly got killed in the middle of the night. I'm going."

Broderick drew a sharp breath to say more, then he looked into Mason's eyes and stopped. Big brother observed him a while, always seeming to know what Mason was thinking. Finally, he gave him a nod. "Fine. You can come with me. But keep quiet unless Liam asks you a direct question."

"I'm not afraid of Liam, the big bad Feline," Mason said, but that wasn't strictly true. Liam had a way of looking at a Shifter with his quiet blue eyes before putting him in his place without twitching a finger. Liam could be extraordinarily generous, and his mate and cub loved him to distraction, but there was no doubt that Liam ran the Austin Shiftertown with a firm paw.

The meeting took place at the bar Liam managed just on the edge of Shiftertown, which didn't open for business until later in the day. Liam was already there by the time Broderick and Mason walked in. He sat calmly on a barstool, one elbow resting on the bar behind him. Shifters weren't allowed to own businesses, so this tavern belonged to a human, but it was clear that Liam was in charge.

Sean, Liam's brother and Andrea's mate, walked in just behind Broderick and Mason, the Sword of the Guardian sticking up over Sean's shoulder. The sword unnerved Mason. A few months ago, Broderick had found a medallion from another Guardian's sword, and the medallion had not only burned a mark on Broderick's palm but sort of stuck with him like a lost puppy. It had done other weird things too, and because of it, Mason, for a time, had thought his brother lost forever. He'd never told Broderick how empty and grief-stricken that had made him feel. Broderick's head was already big enough.

Liam regarded Mason with his dark blue eyes as though trying to decide how culpable Mason was in Aleck's attack. Sean, with the same dark blue eyes as Liam, gave Mason a similar look. Mason growled and slumped down into a chair. He still hurt, his mind fuzzy from the painkillers.

A few other Shifters sat here and there throughout the room. They were Liam's trackers—bodyguards, fighters, scouts—who generally helped Liam find trouble and keep the peace.

"Close the door," Liam said as soon as Broderick had gotten himself up on a barstool. The huge Kodiak bear Shifter, Ronan, who was the bar's bouncer, shut and locked the door.

"So then," Liam began in a calm voice. "It seems Aleck has become a bit of a problem."

"A *bit* of a problem?" Mason heard the snarl leave his mouth before he could stop it. Must be the painkillers—he'd never have interrupted Liam otherwise.

"A *bit*," Liam repeated as Broderick tried to glare Mason to silence. "The poor lad's nearly gone, but he's got a mate and a cub on the way. If it comes down to finishing Aleck off, what becomes of his cub? Of Nancy?"

"Nancy's human," Mason said, unable to keep his mouth shut. "She and Joanne have a family to take care of her."

"True," Liam conceded. "But what human family will want to raise a Shifter cub? They are a handful, to say the least." Liam shook his head but his voice took on a note of pride. He now had a baby Feline daughter who had him wrapped around her tiny fingers. "Nancy's sister is Broderick's mate, so your family, Mason, will have the keeping of Nancy and her cub, if she wishes, but the cub will be clanless."

The Shifters in the room moved restlessly in sympathy. A Shifter without a clan was in a precarious position—they had no natural protectors from the bad world or even from other Shifters. They'd be at the bottom of whatever pack or pride were kind enough to take them in, and finding a mate would be tough. Shifters had a taboo about breeding within their own clan, no matter how very distant the blood connection happened to be. If a Shifter's clan was unknown, other Shifters, especially of their own species, would be very reluctant to take them as mate.

Broderick shrugged as though none of this concerned him. "We can make the cub an honorary member of our clan and take care of him. Or her. That won't be a problem. Even though the cub will be a Feline."

He said *Feline* like an insult, and Liam, a Feline with a lot of lion in him, gave Broderick a tiny smile.

"All right, so Nancy and the cub will have protectors," Liam went on. "But how do we tell the cub that we decided to kill his dad?"

Broderick returned Liam's look with a bland one of his own. "Easy. I'll send him to *you* when he's old enough and have you explain."

"Is killing him the only way?" Mason interrupted as Liam gave Broderick another of his tolerant smiles. "The guy sliced me open, yeah, but it's not his fault he's crazy. Can we just keep him seriously tranqued until he gets better?"

Sean answered. "No, lad. From what Andrea and I have learned, the feral state eats into your brain—changes the chemistry and synapses. If we can't bring Aleck back soon, he'll have permanent brain damage. Then he'll be a danger not only to the Lupines he smells around him but to his own mate. We can't let that happen."

"So we off him?" Mason said. "Doesn't seem fair. Shifters have been brought back from the feral state before, right?"

Mason didn't know why he had this sudden rush of compassion for Aleck. The man had been raving and drooling more or less the whole time he'd lived in Mason's family home. In his lucid periods, Aleck had been clear that he was grateful to them but didn't much like Lupines, or any Collared Shifters at all. Dickhead. Must be Mason's painkillers making him soft.

Sean said, "If he's not too far gone, a healer could bring him back. *If* we can find a healer."

"Your mate," Mason said at once. "She healed *me*." He waved a hand at his abdomen, which still hurt.

One of the trackers, nodded. "Yeah, she has a fine touch."

Sean's eyes narrowed and a growl left his throat. He went from concerned Guardian to possessive mate so fast that Mason laughed out loud.

"Peace," Liam rumbled, putting a calming hand on his brother's arm. "He's teasing you, Sean, and easy it is to do. No, lad," he said to Mason. "Andrea's a healer, but her gift comes from her Fae blood. Sean means a *Shifter* healer, one that's blessed by the Goddess with a strong amount of healing magic. A Shifter healer, it is said, can bring another Shifter back almost from the dead. They're powerful, rare, and extremely elusive. If I knew where I could get my hands on one, I would."

"That's it, then." Mason slapped the arms of his chair and pried himself to his feet. He swayed on those feet, still feeling the effects of his healing and the painkillers. "I'll go find us a Shifter healer, and we'll be done with this problem once and for all."

Chapter Two

The others argued. Of course they did — they were Shifters.

Mason had already made up his mind. He was going no matter what. He didn't think it was prudent to say this to Liam, so he simply slid himself into a booth in the corner and let them babble.

"Hey." A Feline Shifter took the opposite seat and rested his forearms on the table. He was Seamus McGuire, who'd not long ago been part of a compound of Shifters, the same Aleck had belonged to, who'd managed to avoid taking the Collar twenty years ago. Seamus wore a fake Collar now, its Celtic knot nestled on his throat. He'd agreed to live like a Shiftertown Shifter to be with a woman — a human woman at that.

The man had to be seriously nuts. If Mason hadn't had a Collar he sure as hell wouldn't hang around here. No woman was worth captivity, even pretend captivity.

"Aleck was a friend," Seamus said, his slow voice holding a Scottish bite. "I wasn't best mates with him or anything, but he's not a bad lad. I appreciate you wanting to help him."

Mason wanted to help Aleck to keep from being killed by him. He kept this thought to himself and waited for Seamus to get to the point.

"If you truly want to find a Shifter healer, you're going to need help," Seamus said.

"Possibly," Mason responded, cautious. "Are you volunteering to go with me?"

Seamus gave him an incredulous look. "Tell my mate and her mother that I'm going to scour the world for a healer while my mate is carrying my cub? You've met Bree's mum."

Mason had, and agreed that she was an alpha in her own right. A Shifter didn't piss off Nadine Fayette unless he wanted a takedown that burned like fire. She'd remind said Shifter of the incident every time she saw him too, such as when Mason had torn through her rosebushes when he'd been chasing a cub at the last cookout Bree and her family had held at their house. Mason could still feel the scratches of thorns and Nadine's lashing voice. He'd replanted the bushes he'd broken and driven out there to check on them until he was sure they were thriving.

"So what do you suggest?" Mason asked impatiently.

Seamus started to take on an irritated, exhausted, and pained appearance, matching Mason's feelings exactly. Seamus was an empath, and when other Shifters exuded strong emotions, Seamus would pick up on them and reflect them. This gave him the ability to help the Shifter get over the bad emotion, or something like that. Mason wasn't clear on why being an empath was a good thing.

"Bree has a friend in New Orleans," Seamus said as he held Mason with his golden gaze. "One with resources."

"What resources?" Mason asked. "Better than the Guardian Network?"

"No." Seamus flushed. "Sean says the Guardian Network can point the way toward a Shifter healer but not exactly where to find him. Healers can be elusive. No, Bree's friend is a psychic."

Mason regarded him with a slow blink, anger seeping into the mix in his brain. "Are you fucking kidding me?"

Seamus lifted a hand. "I know it sounds weird, but Bree says she's amazing. She's found people for the police, has warned others of danger in time for them to save themselves, other stuff. I don't believe in psychics meself, but Bree swears she's the real thing."

Bree, while a cute enough human woman, wasn't herself the most reliable source. She'd been a Shifter groupie when she'd lived in New Orleans, and any woman who thought that hanging out with asshole alpha male Shifters was a wonderful thing had to have her head examined. And now Seamus was telling him Bree believed in psychics.

"Pass," Mason said. "Got any other ideas?"

"No harm in asking her," Seamus said. "Who knows? She might at least point you in the right direction."

"There's no such thing as psychics," Mason said stubbornly. "They're frauds who use your body language to 'read' your mind. Any Shifter can do that. If this woman finds people, she's either a good investigator on the quiet, or she got lucky. Same with warning of impending disaster. There are disasters galore out there, every day. Any psychic has a good chance of predicting one."

"So what?" Seamus said. "By your argument, if she's a good investigator, she might be able to help you." He leaned across the table, his golden eyes sharp. "Let me put it this way, lad. If I go home and tell Bree you didn't want to meet her friend, both Bree and Nadine will come out here, round you up, and drag you off to New Orleans themselves. You want a road trip like that? Easier if you volunteer to go on your own."

Mason let his growls rumble. "Seamus, why the hell do you let a bunch of *females* tell you what to do? They're not even Shifter."

Seamus lost his annoyance and let out a laugh, his pained expression clearing. "Tell you what, lad, the day you fall in love, you come back to me and ask me that again."

Mason pressed his hands on the tabletop to keep from balling his fists. "All right, all right." New Orleans was a nice distance from Austin, and Mason felt an urge to get out of town. He could talk to the psychic to make Seamus and his family happy, take a few breaths away from the chaos that was his home, and decide what he wanted to do.

Mason became aware that all the other Shifters in the room were watching him. Shifter hearing being what it was, they'd likely followed the whole conversation.

"It's settled then," Liam Morrissey said. His eyes glinted with humor but also understanding. "You go find us a Shifter healer, lad. We'll keep Aleck alive until you get home."

***

Jasmine Samuelson stared at the rune stones she'd just cast on her blue velvet cloth, and her heart constricted. She shoved the stones aside, took out her personal tarot deck—the one she used to read for herself and no one else—and quickly dealt three cards in a row.

She sat back and sucked in a breath. Jazz called this deal her "quickie" tarot—the first card was her past; the second, the present; third, her immediate future. The wind chimes outside the veranda door sighed, though there was no wind.

Every rune she'd drawn and every tarot layout for the past few days had told her much the same thing. Even the fortune cookies she'd had when she'd ordered Chinese takeout the other night had warned of it.

A stranger was coming. When he arrived, Jasmine's entire life would change. Forever.

Jazz wasn't opposed to strangers—she made her living working in a New Age shop in town, and she read palms and tarot for those she didn't know all the time. She enjoyed it, meeting all kinds of interesting people who had all kinds of interesting problems.

She wasn't opposed to change either. Life shouldn't be stagnant.

What Jazz was opposed to were dire portents laid out in her cards that this stranger would scare the shit out of her, and change her life in a massive way.

It was enough to make her call in sick at work, close all the shutters in her house on the river, and hide in the shadows.

The house embraced and protected her, full of magic from many generations of magic-touched women and men, stretching back to the eighteenth century. Her boyfriend, Lucas, didn't understand why Jazz wouldn't let him move in here, but the truth was that the house didn't like him.

Hanging out with Lucas could be a lot of fun, when he was having a good week, and he'd been bugging her for them to move in together. But that either meant Jazz leaving the house that had been her home most of her life or having Lucas come to live here. She'd have to face him sooner or later with her final decision, which might mean that she and Lucas would break up.

Maybe that's what the coming stranger meant. The end of her relationship, or perhaps Jazz having to move out of her house.

Is that all I'm afraid of? Jazz admonished herself after she hung up from telling the shop's manager she wasn't coming in. *A breakup or a move? A lot of people go through so much worse.* But leaving this house wasn't simply a move to a new building and she knew it. Jazz's past was here. Her present. Her future?

She sat down again in the dining room and shuffled the cards, slowly dealing out the Celtic cross. She studied each card as she laid it down, then contemplated the entire spread when she was finished.

Yep, something scary was coming. Jazz shoved the cards together then sat back and curled her fingers into nervous fists.

A second later, her cell phone rang. Jazz's heart jumped high as she grabbed for it, then she let out a relieved breath when she saw who it was.

"Bree!" she cried into the phone. "I can't tell you how glad I am to hear from you ..."

***

Mason's shirt stuck to his chest as his motorcycle took him through the wet heat of southern Louisiana on his way into New Orleans. Early this morning, he'd ridden out of Austin toward Houston on the back highways, a hoodie zipped up to conceal his Collar. Shifters were allowed to travel within their own state, as long as they didn't stay outside their own Shiftertown too long, but Mason didn't need anyone noticing a Shifter sliding out the other side of Houston and on down the road into Louisiana.

Now the heat of the afternoon clung to him, the sun blaring through thin white clouds, the humidity soaring. Austin could be humid in the summer, but nothing like this. It was like riding through soup.

Mason was heading to see Bree's psychic with very little information to go on in his search. According to Sean, the Guardian Network only indicated that three Shifters in the world were genuine Shifter healers. No names or addresses of course, though the database indicated they were male. One had last been seen somewhere in the Baltic countries. Another hung out in South America. A third drifted around the United States and Canada. All of them wandered, never staying in any one place long.

Healers did that, apparently. They were elusive, reclusive, and reputed to be nearly as crazy as ferals. Goddess-touched, Sean called them, as were the Guardians, but healers brought people back to life instead of sending them to death.

The healing magic messed up their brains, Sean went on, and they didn't like to be around other Shifters. Or anyone, for that matter. A Shifter had to be truly desperate to search for one.

Mason tightened his grip on the handlebars, his fingerless gloves stretching. It was too hot for anything but the muscle shirt he wore beneath the hoodie, but he kept the jacket zipped to his chin.

The I-10 took him through hot green lands to industrial areas alongside the wide river. Then the freeway skimmed a huge lake to finally spill him into the heart of New Orleans.

Mason followed Bree's directions to a place called Jackson Square, a green area with a big church, crowds of tourists, and slow-moving, horse-drawn carriages taking said tourists around the old town. Mason moved his bike leisurely through the traffic to Decatur Street, gazing like any tourist at the old city with its stuccoed walls and intricate wrought-iron balconies.

Mason rode around a corner from Decatur into a tiny street, killed the bike, and approached the shop called *Inspirations*, where Bree told Mason her friend Jasmine worked.

Two young women in halter tops and shorts were heading into the store at the same time. Mason yanked the door out of the first woman's grip and ducking past her into the shop to scope it out for danger.

The shop's interior looked innocuous enough. It was small but held many shelves and display cases filled with books, stones of all colors, statues and figurines, bottles of oil, decks of cards, jewelry, crystals, incense burners and incense, and various and sundry objects whose function Mason couldn't determine.

He turned back to the women and stepped aside to let them in, nodding at them to let them know it was safe.

The first one glared at him. "I guess no one learns *manners* these days. How rude."

The second was about to agree with her friend, then she looked up at Mason and halted, her eyes softening as she smiled. Mason had seen that smile from human women before, one that said they wouldn't mind anything he did and kind of hoped they'd end up somewhere private.

So—one woman was disgusted at Mason for being protective, and the other wanted to rush off alone with a guy she'd never met.

Human females were seriously crazy.

Mason did his best to ignore them as he approached the counter. He didn't see any "No Shifters" signs, but he kept his Collar hidden, just in case.

The woman at the cash register was folding up silk scarves to place on a display. She glanced up as Mason reached her, did a double take, and dropped the scarf.

Mason caught it for her, the silk soft against his rough fingertips. "Hey," he said in a low voice. "I'm looking for Jasmine."

The woman kept on staring, ignoring the scarf Mason held out to her. "Is she here?" Mason prompted, shoving the cloth closer to the woman.

The woman jumped. "Jazz? No. She's not here. Not today."

"Do you know where she is, then? I need to find her."

Another jump. Mason wasn't good at guessing human ages, but the woman had lines on her face and gray in her hair, and was very slender. She wore a flowing, thin silk jacket over a wispy shirt, probably wise in this climate. Mason's hoodie was stifling him.

"No," the woman said. "I can't tell you that. You'd better go."

She made no move to take the scarf from him, and in fact, looked scared to death. Mason heard the two women come up behind him. The one who'd said he was rude asked, "Do you want me to call the police?"

That was all Mason needed. If he ran from the cops, they'd chase him, maybe shoot him, and then peel his jacket back from his bloody body to see his Collar. Then it would be Shifter Bureau, a cage, and possible death. Broderick, as Mason's alpha, would be arrested for letting Mason out of his control, and then Liam would get hauled in for not keeping a Shifter in his Shiftertown inside the state lines.

How did Liam, Seamus, Ronan, Spike—all the Shifters mated to humans—deal with them? Their human mates looked at them and melted. Even Nancy, mated to a feral, for the Goddess's sake, was ready to do anything to save him.

Mason cleared his throat and tried to quirk his lips into a smile. Charm came so easy for Liam and Sean, but Mason had to work at it. Maybe it was their Irish accent. Women loved accents.

Mason wasn't foolish enough to try one. He said in his own, plain-old voice, "I'll buy this scarf then. For my auntie Cora. She likes scarves."

The woman behind the counter softened the slightest bit at the mention of his aunt. "Do you want a box for it?" she asked.

"No, no. I'll just …" Mason looked at the piece of cloth, not knowing what to do with the thing.

The woman's mouth now blossomed into a smile. "I'll wrap it up real nice for her." She rummaged on a shelf below the counter and brought out tissue and a folded box, then tapped keys on her register. "That comes to eighty-two fifty-nine."

Mason felt the growl in his throat but suppressed it. Small price to pay to keep these people from giving him to the cops. He hid his grimace with another smile, dug out cash from his pocket, and laid it down.

A few minutes later, he walked out carrying a gray-and-black striped bag with *Inspirations* on it, which contained a slim box wrapped in colorful paper, a brochure about the store, and a complimentary stick of incense.

As he mounted his motorcycle, he saw the two women plus the woman from the register at the door watching him. The door was closed, but his Shifter hearing picked up what they were saying.

"Doesn't he look like Orlando Bloom?" the woman who'd called him rude asked.

Sudden excitement tinged the voices of the others. "You think it's him?" "Yeah, he does look like him." "Yeah, I bet that's him!"

Mason started his bike, lifted his hand in farewell, and eased out into the narrow street.

"I swear to you — that was Orlando Bloom ..."

Mason let out the snarl that had been building in his throat. Whoever this Bloom guy was, Mason felt sorry for him.

He was about to pull into traffic on the main street again when his coat vibrated. Mason stopped the bike to pull out his phone.

"What?" he shouted into it.

"That's how you answer the phone?" The voice of Bree came at him. "I've been trying to call you all day, Mason, but I couldn't reach you."

"I've been on the road. Your friend isn't at her store." Mason couldn't keep his irritation at bay. "What do I do now? Hire a psychic to find *her*?"

Bree snorted. "Don't be a smart-ass. That's what I've been trying to call to tell you. Jazz stayed home today, but I know where she lives ..."

***

Jazz stood on the front porch of the graceful house and watched the biker come up the drive. Bree had warned her, but Jazz's heart banged like crazy, her blood cold as he rode slowly under the stately trees and turned the bike to stop it right below the porch.

The stranger who would change her life.

Well, no one could be stranger than a Shifter. Jazz had vowed never to have anything to do with them again, and now here she was, agreeing to see one as a favor to an old friend.

Mason McNaughton, Bree had said his name was. A little wild, even for a Shifter, but he needed to hire Jasmine. Needed her help.

Just another client, Jazz told herself. She drew a steadying breath and straightened up as Mason swung himself off the bike, unzipped his hoodie, and headed for the porch.

When he put his foot on the bottom step, the whole house trembled. Mason stopped, looked around quickly as though he'd felt that, and snapped his gaze to Jasmine's.

He had wolf's eyes. Gray and piercing, they could have been contemplating fleeing prey on moonlit grasslands. Sunlight touched dark hair that had been cut short, burning gold highlights into it.

"You the psychic?" he asked. His voice was low, rumbling, and held disbelief.

Jazz folded her arms. "I am. Are you the Shifter?"

Mason looked over the house, which rose three stories above them, then he took a long inhalation, as though testing the air. "I'm Mason. Bree called you?"

"She said you wanted to hire me." Jazz forced her voice to take on its professional tones. *Just another client.* "If you'll follow me, I'll talk to you in the gazebo."

She walked briskly to the open double front door with stained glass sidelights. Beyond was a wide, breezy hallway that would take them straight through the house and out to the back veranda.

Mason was next to Jazz before she could walk inside. She halted, drawing a quick breath, as Mason's warm, hard body blocked the doorway.

His aura almost knocked her over. Jazz had seen the hint of it as he'd approached the house, the animal overlaid with the man.

Now that he was right next to her, Mason's aura shoved everything else aside and took over. The psychic cloud around him was gray, like his eyes, but shot through with glowing gold.

He looked at her with those wolf eyes that told her he could rip away all her psychic defenses and open up her soul. He'd take what he needed from her and then leave her exhausted, gasping, and terrified.

Mason didn't say a word, but his brows drew together as though wondering why she was standing there gaping at him. His hair, entirely dark now in the shadows, was messy from riding, and his body bulked under jeans, T-shirt, and light fleece jacket. The Collar that told the world without doubt that he was Shifter winked in the hollow of his throat.

Without waiting for Jazz to speak or explain, Mason strode into the house, looking around in wariness, then held out a hand when she tried to follow him in.

"Stop," he said, the word forceful. "There is danger here."

Chapter Three

"What?" The psychic hurried in behind Mason without obeying his command. "What the hell are you talking about?"

Humans were like that. They rushed into danger and then got mad at Shifters for trying to keep them out of it.

There was something weird about this house. Mason could smell it, the hovering strength waiting to crush if necessary, protecting or rejecting, as it decided.

Houses didn't have personalities, Mason told himself. Although, now that he thought about it, the one he lived in had an atmosphere of warmth and disorder, a messy kind of comfort. This house had seen gladness, pain, grief, death, life, and now bore an emptiness overlaid with a faint sadness.

"You live here by yourself?" he asked Jasmine.

"Yeah. Why?"

Mason looked down the wide hallway. Open from front door to back, the hall was paneled in polished, gleaming wood that had a deep red tone. Mahogany, probably, but very old. Doors, closed, lined it, and a staircase, set at a right angle to the large hall, led upward to dimly lit floors. In spite of the humid heat outside, a cool breeze filled the passageway.

Jasmine herself was like a cool breeze. She had black hair, which didn't look naturally black, cut short, the ends jagged against her cheeks. A tank top outlined her curved torso, and her skirt ended at mid-thigh, baring a long length of leg. Painted toenails peeked out from her sandals, and the same color stained the ends of her fingers. Another weird thing humans did. Why would anyone paint their claws?

A colorful tattoo snaked up her left arm, a flowering vine that crept across her chest to end above her breast. Or did it? One vine dipped under her shirt. To encircle her nipple? Mason found himself trying to peer under the neckline of her tank top to see.

Jasmine noticed. Her mouth firmed. "The gazebo is this way." She pointed at the back door then marched down the hall toward the square of sunlight at the end.

Her hips swayed under the skirt, her legs beckoning Mason's attention. Her body was open and enticing, but her rigid walk said clearly — *I don't like Shifters, so don't touch me.*

Fine. Whatever. Mason wasn't here for pleasure — he was here to get directions to a Shifter healer so the crazy feral at his house would stop trying to kill him.

He cast another glance up the stairs as he passed by and then looked at the corbeled ceiling above him. He held up his hands to whatever presence he felt here. *Peace. I only want to talk to her. I'll pay her fee without quibbling and go away.*

A gust of wind burst through the hall, making Jasmine's skirt dance as she exited. Windows upstairs rattled, the staircase creaked, doors shook in their frames, and the chandelier that hung from the top of the house wobbled. Mason felt a breath of emotion touch him, but it held mirth rather than anger.

This was so not right. Mason hurried to catch up with Jasmine and let out a breath when he made it to the back porch and the brightness of the afternoon.

The gazebo, Mason saw, wasn't a separate building, but a piece of the veranda that jutted out from the far right side of the porch. It ran a long way into the yard, seven of its eight sides exposed to the sunshine, the last side of the octagon open to the veranda.

White painted lattices, railings, and what he'd heard called gingerbread decorated the gazebo. A wooden table from another century with chairs to match stood in the middle of it, and low shelves around the walls held flowering plants. A rose vine snaked around the outside of the lattices, red and pink roses just beginning to bloom. Books and small boxes filled another shelf.

In one corner, on a stand, stood a guitar. Mason's interested gaze went to it at once.

"Do you play?" he asked.

Jasmine glanced at the guitar as though she'd forgotten its existence, then she flushed, suddenly shy. "A little. Not very well." She shook herself, abruptly businesslike. "Please take a seat, Mr. McNaughton. I've been expecting your visit."

Mason pulled his attention from the guitar. It was a vintage Martin, a great instrument, maybe from the 1950s. In seriously good shape too, though worn from playing, which would only enhance the sound. This guitar had been treasured.

He flicked his gaze back to Jasmine. She had blue eyes, deeply blue, like the depths of a Texas lake.

"Why?" he asked skeptically. "Did you see it in your crystal ball?"

She made a face. "Very funny. I've heard all the psychic jokes — trust me. The snide questions about why I haven't won the lottery or why I don't bet on the Super Bowl. I meant that I knew that you, specifically, were coming, because Bree told me. But, yeah, I did see in the cards and any other augury I cast that I would have an unusual visitor." Jasmine's lips thinned as though the things she'd seen hadn't pleased her. "What is it you need my help with?"

Mason lowered himself into a chair as Jasmine sat on the opposite side of the table. She took one of the intricately carved wooden boxes from the shelf, extracted a blue velvet cloth that matched her eyes, and carefully spread the cloth across the middle of the table.

Mason placed his hands on the table's wooden edge. As he did, the porch floor vibrated beneath his feet and the wind chimes moved, though the breeze had completely died. His wolf's hackles rose.

"You sure there's no one else here?" He sniffed the air but detected only roses, old wood, and Jasmine, who smelled a little like ... jasmine.

"I'm sure," Jasmine said. She rested her hand, palm up, on the cloth. In Shifter terms, that was a gesture of openness, showing she wasn't a danger and could be trusted. In human terms—who the hell knew? "The house is seriously haunted, but I'm the only *person* living here now."

"Haunted," Mason repeated. "Right."

"I don't mean with ghosts stalking up and down the halls or skeletons groaning in the cellar. I mean the house itself. It's old and has been through a lot. Life, death, slavery, war, happiness, sadness, abandonment, neglect. I inherited it when my grandmother died last year, and though everyone advised me to sell it or turn it into a hotel, I decided I'd stay here and take care of it." Jasmine glanced past Mason at the length of the veranda and the house's many windows lined with dark green shutters. "The house seems happy with my decision."

Mason followed her gaze, taking in the house, then the few outbuildings—garage, what looked like a workshop of some kind, a small piece of garden, a few tiny cottages, a thick hedge, and more giant trees. Beyond the trees, he could see industrial buildings and the intrusive yellow arm of a crane. The house might once have been a stately home on a big farm on the river, but the world had moved on. Now the estate was a tiny island in the industrial heart of the Mississippi.

"*My* house was never asked if it liked us," Mason said, turning to the table again. "We were just told to live there. The house had to suck it up."

The corners of Jasmine's mouth twitched, which softened her face. "Does it like you now?"

Mason shrugged. "I don't know. It's bursting at the seams. There's me, Broderick, Corey, Derek, Aunt Cora, and now Aleck, Nancy, and Joanne. Nancy and Joanne are both pregnant, so soon there will be two cubs running around in the mix."

Jasmine's eyes widened, but he caught a wistfulness in her look. "I don't know if I can wrap my brain around that. I need a lot of quiet time away from people or I go kind of crazy. Too much psychic residue."

Sure, the unbeliever in Mason said. The Shifter in him acknowledged that it was quiet here. Peaceful. The industrial world on the other side of the trees didn't intrude, as though there was a shield around the place. He could rest here. Breathe.

"I need your hand," Jasmine said, wriggling her fingers.

Mason looked at her outstretched palm waiting on the cloth. "What for? I only want you to help me find a guy."

"Yes, I know. But I need to know about *you* before I can answer your questions."

"Why?" Mason studied her in grave suspicion.

Jasmine gave him an impatient look. "It's part of my process. If you're not interested, you can go back to Inspirations and make an appointment with someone else. I'll still have to charge you forty bucks for wasting my time."

Mason frowned at her. "You this cranky with all your woo-woo clients?"

"Only the ones who deride what I do and become major pains in the ass," Jasmine said loftily. "I'm doing this as a favor to Bree—mostly because I feel sorry for her having to live with a Shifter. Now, either lay your hand on the table or go away."

Mason flashed back to his conversation with Seamus only yesterday, when Mason had made fun of him for letting females boss him around. Human ones at that.

Mason let out a sigh, tugged off his right glove, and slapped his hand face down on the cloth. Jasmine grabbed it and turned it over.

Her fingertips were smooth and cool as she skimmed diagonally across his palm. The touch was light, tickling, almost erotic. Mason's heart sped and his skin heated, sweat beading on his upper lip. It sure was hot this afternoon.

"Interesting." Jasmine lost the edge to her voice as she bent closer to Mason's hand. Mason gazed at the crown of her head, noting that the hair at the roots was a chocolate brown that blended into the black. A nice color. She had no need to cover it up.

"What's interesting?" Mason asked.

"You do a lot of work with your hands. Hard work." Her fingertips moved to the base of his thumb and the calluses there. "But this ..." She brushed the crease that arced downward in the middle of his palm. "The way this line curves shows creativity. Lots of it. So does your aura." She glanced at the air above his head as though seeing something there. "What do you do for a living?"

"I work at a warehouse," Mason answered readily. "Hauling around pallets. I'm a Shifter. Not allowed to do a lot of creative work, but the foremen like Shifter strength."

Jasmine gave him a steady look. "Aren't you going to say *You're the psychic. You figure it out?*"

"I think psychic power is bullshit," Mason said without changing expression. "I don't have time to wait around for you to guess. For the creative thing, I'm a luthier."

Jasmine's brows drew together. "A what?"

"Luthier." Mason pronounced the word carefully. "Someone who makes guitars. It comes from the word *lute*. I also make music boxes. Mostly I decorate the box itself — inlaid wood. My brother makes the gears and cylinders."

Jasmine's lips parted in surprise. "Really? That's … cool."

Mason shrugged. "My family's done it for generations. We sell custom-made stuff for extra money."

"Is that why you asked me about my guitar?"

Mason nodded. "It's a Martin. A 00-18 — I'd say 1958 or 59."

Jasmine turned her head to look at the instrument. "It was my grandmother's. She was really good — she taught me how to play a few things."

"She took care of it," Mason said.

"She did. And of her house. And of me. She took me in when I was a teenager, after my parents were killed." Jasmine jerked back to the table, her cheekbones pink. "I'm supposed to be talking about you."

"It's part of *my* process," Mason said calmly. "Now, can you help me find this guy or not?"

Jasmine folded her fingers into her hand and didn't touch Mason again. Too bad. Mason had liked her gentle caress, the way his blood had warmed in the wake of her fingertips.

"Who is it you're looking for?" she asked.

Mason shrugged. "I don't have any idea. He's a Shifter and he lives in either Canada or the United States. I don't know where, and I don't know his name."

Jasmine stared. "Well, that's not helpful. Do you at least know what he looks like?"

"Nope. Never laid eyes on the man. Don't even know what kind of Shifter he is."

Jasmine pinched the bridge of her nose. "Wait, wait, wait. You don't know his name or what he looks like, only that he's somewhere in the U.S. or Canada. And you expect me to look into a crystal ball and find him?"

Mason deflated. "Yeah, I know it sounds stupid. It *is* stupid. But Bree said you could find anyone. So, go ahead. Find him."

Jasmine brought both her hands down to the table. "If you think it's a bad idea, why did you come? You don't believe I can do it, do you?"

"No, I don't." Mason saw no reason to hide the truth. "I'm here because Bree was all excited about sending me to you, because I'm desperate enough to ride halfway across Texas and most of the way through Louisiana to see if you can help, and because I don't want to be home at the moment. Your creepy house full of weird sounds isn't as scary as waking up in the night with a stinking Feline tearing the hell out of your gut."

Mason dropped his hand to his abdomen. Though the wounds were mostly healed, thanks to Andrea and Mason's own metabolism, the remembered pain lingered. Fucking Feline.

Jasmine's blue eyes rounded. "I saw pain edging your aura—and trauma. Is that what happened to you?"

"Yeah, that happened to me. I rode five hundred miles—so I can sleep tonight without worrying about waking up fighting for my life."

"Oh." Jasmine's tongue came out to wet her lower lip, which made it moist and red. "So, where are you staying?"

"I don't know," Mason said irritably. "I haven't thought that far yet. There's a Shiftertown around here, right?"

"West and south of here. On the way to Thibodaux. It will take you a while to get out there, though, and it will be well past dark before you make it." Jasmine looked at his hands again, one still gloved. "Shifters aren't supposed to go to other Shiftertowns, are they?" She hesitated. "You could always crash here."

Mason regarded her flushed face in surprise. Was she propositioning him? Some human females, like the groupies, would do anything for a shag with a Shifter, though Mason had never obliged. He'd sensed that the quieter of the women at the New Age store today had been more than willing.

Jasmine didn't look the same as the women who sidled up to Mason and his brothers at Shifter bars, looking for a night in the sack. Mason always turned them down, not liking their self-seeking grasping. Jasmine made the offer nervously, as though she felt obligated to offer hospitality and hoped Mason would say no.

Under his steady gaze, Jasmine's flush deepened. "There's a bunk in the workshop over there." She waved her hand at the outbuildings. "I have to keep this place up if I want it listed as a historic home and let tourists pay to see it, so sometimes the carpenters sleep there while they're restoring things."

"In other words, you're just being polite," Mason said.

"I was raised to be courteous," Jasmine said coolly. "If you're caught outside your state, you'll be arrested, right? I really do want to find out more about you and see if I can help you. I'm interested." She tightened her lips. "Professionally, I mean. Don't worry, I'll lock my doors."

Mason huffed a laugh. "I'm not interested in human women, sweetheart. And I don't want to stay in your weird-ass house, believe me." The floorboards vibrated again, as though the place laughed at him.

"It likes you," Jasmine said in surprise. "The house I mean. It doesn't like everyone."

"Oh good," Mason rumbled. "A building that thinks I'm cool."

"It's not usually that bad. It's just acting up today for some reason."

Jasmine said the words offhand, but Mason saw the worry in her. She knew damn well why the house was on edge, but she wasn't going to share the knowledge.

The sun was already low in the west, and the thought of riding out through the sticky city and all its traffic to find another Shiftertown, where the Shifters would regard him with wariness even as they took him in, didn't appeal to him. Mason could sleep in the wood shop—he liked wood shops—fix Jasmine breakfast in the morning as a thank you, and head back out again, continuing his search for the healer.

"Sure, I'll stay," Mason said. "If you play something for me on that guitar. I'd like to hear how it sounds."

Jasmine started, then turned to study the instrument. "If you make guitars, why don't you play it for *me*?"

"Because I suck at it," Mason said. "I know how to work the wood, get a nice sound, play some notes and chords. That's it. I'm not a musician."

"Neither am I," Jasmine answered, a little ruefully. "I'm warning you. I only know what my grandmother taught me."

Mason shrugged. "Whatever. Just strum it or something. I don't care."

She was going to refuse. Mason didn't know why he wanted her to play for him, but he suddenly wanted it with everything he had. A woman, sexy in her limbs-baring clothes, running her fingers over an amazing guitar, her touch as light as it had been on his hand … Oh, wait. Mason knew exactly why he wanted her to play.

Jasmine looked uncertain, but she reached for the Martin. She lifted the strap over her shoulder, smoothed her skirt, and rested the guitar on her lap.

"My grandmother liked old jazz." Jasmine smiled in memory as she fingered the strings with her left hand and lightly strummed with her right. "That's why she always called me Jazz."

Jazz was too short and snappy for this woman, Mason decided. He preferred *Jasmine* — slower, more delicate.

"She liked blues too," Jasmine went on. "Loved Albert King. No way can I play like that." She laughed softly.

Mason watched her transform from a guarded, nervous, and watchful woman, mistrustful of Mason and wishing he'd go away, to nostalgic, smiling, and at ease—simply by setting an old guitar in her lap and smoothing its strings. It was amazing what music and instruments did for people.

Jasmine strummed an A minor, stopping to flick her little finger on a few single notes on the B string, and then she began to sing.

Mason had no idea what the song was. It was slow and sweet, languid like the river flowing past them—or as the river had been before the docks and big tankers had invaded. The song was about a lover waiting in the moonlight, hoping her man would come, and knowing he'd betrayed her. Sad, melancholy, and beautiful.

Jasmine struggled with the chords and shook her head as she kept singing. Her voice, though not trained or perfectly true, was a rich alto that was full and nice to listen to. Mason imagined her voice like that in the night when she turned to him and rested her head on his shoulder.

He abruptly killed the image. What the hell was he thinking? Mason wasn't here for seduction, something he wasn't skilled at anyway. He needed information. He doubted Jasmine could help, but he wasn't here to drag her off to bed then rush away first thing in the morning.

He'd want to savor Jasmine, and he didn't have time. Maybe when Mason was finished—had found the healer, fixed Aleck, and got his life back—he could drive out here for a visit. Jasmine would play the Martin for him and tell him more about this bizarre old house.

Mason found himself leaning closer as she continued the song. She did smell like jasmine, sweet and strong. He watched her hand move lithely on the fingerboard, the chords more sure as she continued. The guitar sounded as good as Mason had thought it would — low and mellow, its voice aged like the best wine.

Jasmine's voice matched it. Mason's urgency dropped away, his errand drifting to the back of his mind. He could sit out here in the evening breeze as twilight fell and listen to her play forever ...

The floor shuddered. The windows rattled and the wind chimes began to clang, a rude cacophony to the music of the guitar.

A door slammed somewhere in the house and a voice bellowed, "Jazz? Where are you?"

Mason jumped to his feet, instincts springing to life. He'd been so lulled by Jasmine's music that he'd never sensed or scented the other human approach. That never happened to him. Never. Not since the day his father had been shot.

Mason was turning to face the danger when a man charged out of the back door and onto the veranda. He was dark haired, large, and moving fast. "Jazz?"

The man saw Mason and immediately halted, fists balling. The fury of a male whose territory had been violated flushed his face.

"What the hell is this?" he demanded. He spoke to Jasmine but glared at Mason.

"Lucas." Jasmine was on her feet, the guitar in her hand, fear in her scent. "He's a client."

"Client?" Lucas glowered. "Like hell he is. You see clients at the store."

"I called in sick. He had an emergency …"

Jasmine's words trailed off as Lucas resumed his charge toward the gazebo. Mason got in front of him, snarls forming in his mouth, feeling his eyes go wolf.

The man stared at him, but either the gathering darkness hid Mason's face and Collar or Lucas didn't have the sense to be afraid. He swung his balled-up fist at Mason.

Mason caught the hand in mid blow, easily turning it away. Jasmine cried out in dismay, and damned if she didn't throw herself between Mason and Lucas. Goddess, she was trying to protect *Mason*.

"He's a client!" she shouted at Lucas. "Leave him alone. I need the fee."

"If you'd live with me, you wouldn't need money," Lucas yelled back. "So what are you offering him, sitting out here in the dark, singing to him like a whore?"

Before Mason could push Jasmine aside to stop him, Lucas yanked the Martin out of Jasmine's hands and smashed it over the gazebo's railing.

Chapter Four

Jazz shrieked. Her grandmother's beloved guitar fell in pieces, some landing on the veranda floor, the others raining to the flower beds below. Lucas blinked, as though surprised at himself, then his jaw clenched again.

"Lucas, you total bastard!" Jazz's heart ached while her fury rose.

Lucas recovered his anger swiftly. "Don't blame me for this, you two-timing bit—"

The word broke off as both Jazz and Lucas became aware of the predator on the veranda with them.

Mason's eyes had gone so light gray they were nearly white, stark in the shadows. His body rumbled, the noise coming from his mouth as barely controlled growls. He pinned Lucas with a primal stare, one that said the jackal in his sights had just done a bad, bad thing.

Lucas, the man Jazz had once thought so handsome, who'd swept her off her feet when he'd sauntered into the store a year ago, went slack-jawed with fear. Jazz saw Lucas's true self come to the fore as he gaped at Mason—Lucas was a rather weak man who controlled others to make himself feel better. She had known this in her heart—her psychic senses had told her so—but she'd chosen to ignore the signals in her loneliness.

There was no ignoring Lucas's self-centered arrogance now, or his terror. His aura became a light puce color, wavering.

Mason, on the other hand, was intrinsically strong all the way through. The aura that had nearly knocked Jazz over was solid, unchanged, unfearing. Mason could reach out right now, wrap a hand around Lucas's neck, and easily snap it, and Lucas, deep down in his quivering heart, knew it.

Lucas's voice was a ragged whisper. "Is he ... Shifter?"

Jazz didn't answer. Mason didn't move, and Lucas drew a shaking breath. "He *is* Shifter. He can't threaten me. I'm calling—"

The cell phone Lucas yanked from his pants pocket was dragged out of his hand by powerful fingers. One squeeze and the cell phone became a pile of plastic and chips that pattered to the veranda's wooden floor.

"Get out," Mason said, his voice so raw and guttural it was a shock to hear it from a human throat. "Never seek Jasmine again."

Lucas stared at him a moment, his mouth opening and closing, then as Mason took a step forward, Lucas turned and fled.

"I'm calling the cops!" he yelled as he ran. "You're dead, Shifter."

"No!" Jazz took two steps after him then found herself stopped by a heavy arm around her waist. She swung back to Mason, who was inches from her, his warmth covering her. "Let go. I have to stop him. You can't be arrested. I know what happens to Shifters."

Mason's eyes eased back from furious wolf as he looked at Jasmine in surprise. "It's all right. I'll be far from here by the time they come."

"No." Jasmine clutched his arm, and Mason's perplexed look grew. "I mean, you can't go yet. I need to help you find ... whoever he is."

"Not if it puts you in danger," Mason said.

Arguments Jazz opened her mouth to spout died as she heard Lucas cry out. From inside the house came a loud thud, then a groan.

Jazz and Mason exchanged a look then rushed inside, Mason in the lead.

All was quiet in the now-dark hallway, the breeze that blew through the house gentle. Jazz could see Lucas's truck parked not far from Mason's motorcycle outside, but Lucas was nowhere in sight.

"Lucas?" Jazz called hesitantly.

No answer. Mason moved to look up the staircase. "You have lights in here?"

"Of course I do." Jazz flipped all the wall switches, filling the lower and upper halls with light. The chandelier that hung from the top of the staircase glowed. "Help me look for him."

She began opening doors. The rooms on the lower floor contained furniture either original to the house — well-kept heirlooms or restored finds from the basement—or handmade replicas. These rooms were for the house tours, to show what life on a late eighteenth-century plantation had been like.

Jazz lived on the second floor. Her grandmother had built a kitchen up there so the lower floor could be left in its original configuration, from a time when the kitchen had been a separate building to keep the fires and smells away from the main house. The original kitchen was preserved now, and shown as part of the house tour.

Lucas wasn't in any of the downstairs rooms. Jazz turned on all the lights and checked every corner of the parlor, dining room, library, music room, parlor-bedroom. She hurried back to the staircase hall, where Mason was busy scrutinizing the wide, polished floorboards.

He pressed his foot to a board that rocked on the studs below it. "These are loose."

"I know," Jazz said. "I keep having them repaired, but they come loose again every time. I rope them off on tour days. It's right below the chandelier anyway."

Mason directed his gaze straight up to the ponderous wrought-iron chandelier that had hung from that spot for well over two hundred years. The chandelier had never fallen in all that time, even when storms shook the house; however, it chose that moment to sway.

Mason stepped respectfully back, but he studied the floorboards again. "What's under there?"

"Subfloor," Jazz said, knowing every inch of the house. When a person kept an old place restored, she came to know it intimately. "Below that, basement—not an underground basement—we're too close to the river for that. They built the house up higher to turn the space underneath into a storage area. The root cellar is just under there." She pointed to the first step of the staircase.

Mason's gaze was still on the floor, and Jazz realized he was *sniffing*. Like a dog. Well, a wolf was kind of a dog, right? "Can you get down to it?" he asked.

"Yes, the door's over there." Jazz waved her hand at the end of the hall, where a door inside the back entrance led to a short flight of stairs.

Mason strode past her and down the hall, took hold of the cellar door's handle, and rattled it. "It's locked."

"Shouldn't be," Jazz said, surprised. She grabbed the keys from the drawer of the Duncan Phyfe table in the hall and joined him. "I only lock it on tour days."

She fumbled with the keys, found the right one, and inserted it into the lock. It wouldn't turn. Jazz yanked out the key and stared at it. No, this was the right one. She tried again. "Damn, what is wrong with this thing?"

Mason turned abruptly and strode back to the main staircase hall. Jazz gave up on the lock and followed him.

She found Mason standing on the loose boards, looking all the way up to the chandelier and the beamed ceiling three and a half stories above them. "Hey," he said, speaking carefully. "If he disappears, and Jasmine is taken in for doing something to him, she won't be able to live here anymore."

Jazz stared at him. "You say you don't believe in psychics," she said. "But you'll talk to a *house*?"

Mason shrugged his large shoulders. His hoodie was all the way open now, giving her a glimpse of flesh inside his muscle shirt. "My brother had a sword talking to him for a while. Why not a whole house?"

There was a rumble, a creak of wood, and then Jazz heard a muffled yell. "Hey!" Lucas was calling. "Get me out of here!"

Mason dropped to his knees and started pulling away the floorboards. They came up easily, pried apart by his big hands.

In the cramped spaced between floor and subfloor, they found Lucas lying on his stomach, arms outstretched, fingers moving as though he wanted to dig his way out. His eyes were closed, and he kept shouting.

Mason reached down, closed an arm around Lucas's waist, and hauled him up. Lucas landed on his feet, his eyes still closed, fingers clawing, until Mason shook him.

"Stop it. You're all right."

Lucas peeled open his eyes. He looked at the floorboards then at Jazz and Mason, and then his knees buckled.

Mason caught him before he fell. He stoically lifted Lucas, half conscious and babbling, over his shoulder, and strode out of the house with him. Jazz watched through the open front door as Mason set Lucas in the driver's seat of his truck then stood back and said something to him.

Jazz tried to lift one of the boards into place, but it was heavy, and she dropped it. Mason had moved it as though it weighed nothing. She'd have to call the contractors to fix the floor — *again*.

Suddenly weary, she wandered outside to the veranda. She walked down the steps and retrieved all the pieces of her beloved guitar then returned to the gazebo and sat down, setting the remains of the guitar on the table. The neck had come off, the top and bottom smashed. The strings hung limply from the tuning pegs, and the bridge, detached from the body, dangled on the ends of the strings.

Tears filled her yes. "Damn it."

"Hey."

Mason stood over her. Jazz hadn't heard him come back to the house, not even his step on the veranda. He regarded her with eyes the gray of storm clouds, the wolf fading.

"He's gone," Mason went on. "He won't be bothering you anymore."

"He was my boyfriend!" Jazz said loudly, her anger rising. "All right, so he was a douchebag. My friends all say I have the worst taste in men, and they're right." Her throat ached. "Why would he do this?" She touched the guitar, a broken, dead thing.

Mason crouched down on his heels. He was a big man, so even in that position his head came to her shoulder. He put his fingers next to hers on the guitar. "I'm a luthier. I can fix it for you. It won't be worth as much repaired, but you'll be able to play it."

"I don't care how much it's worth." Jazz glared at him. "It was my grandmother's. I loved that guitar." She let out a sigh. "I'm sorry. I know you're trying to help …"

"Don't be sorry," Mason said in a hard voice. "It's that dickhead's fault, not yours. Don't take other people's idiocy onto yourself."

Jazz opened her mouth to answer, but her words died as Mason leaned to her, coming right into her personal space. Shifters did that, Jazz had come to know. They were much more at ease with bodily contact than humans, and they didn't realize when they were too close for human comfort. Nearness was good for them, apparently. It helped soothe them, let them know that they weren't alone.

Jazz was definitely alone. Mason's presence was nice, cutting the loneliness of the place. Long ago, this house had been alive, people running in and out all the time, children playing, the house full of voices and laughter. One of Jazz's ancestors had been an abolitionist when it hadn't been fashionable to be, gave his slaves papers that said they were free, and rented out the slave quarters to farmers, thus reducing the aura of human misery the place could have had.

But it was lonely. Now that her grandmother was gone, the tourists and Jazz's friends only made so much of a dent in the house's emptiness.

Mason watched her closely, his eyes framed with dark lashes that matched his unruly hair. His lips were firm in his strong face, his jaw brushed with dark whiskers that spoke of his many-hour journey from Austin.

Jazz realized she wanted to kiss him. She tried to rein in the urge, but it wouldn't go away. He smelled of dust and exhaust — road scents — of warmth and the fabric of his jacket.

No more Shifters, she told herself sternly. *Never going through that heartbreak again.*

Her body wasn't listening. Shifters did this, drew a person in despite their best efforts, broke down defenses before they could even be raised.

Jazz leaned down and lightly kissed his lips.

***

Mason jumped. Jasmine's mouth was warm and soft, her lips sweet and enticing. Her breath brushed his cheek, her hair satin smooth against his skin.

Mason's body temperature, already high, jumped to searing. The light pressure of her lips did things to his insides and hardened every muscle. He remained rigid, willing himself not to grab her and yank her to him.

Human groupies had kissed him before, wanting him to wrestle them down and have at them. Jasmine wanted … something else. Mason wasn't sure what, but a quick shag wasn't what she had in mind. He didn't have to be psychic to know that.

Before he could decide how to respond, Jasmine pulled back, her face bright red.

"Oh, shit, I'm sorry. I don't know why I did that. I'm just upset. I—"

Mason cupped the back of her head and pulled her to him, stilling her words. Her lips were parted, and Mason took advantage, sweeping his tongue between them. He tugged at her again, and Jasmine lost her balance and landed against him.

Heat flowed around him, embracing him like a lover. Mason ran his hand down Jasmine's back, catching on her bra beneath her thin shirt. He stopped his touch at her waist, knowing she'd scramble away if he took his hand to her backside. He wasn't ready for her to push away yet, wanting this warm kiss to go on.

Jasmine's heartbeat sped as her breasts crushed against his chest, her pulse high under his fingertips. She tasted fresh like clear water, smelled of the flowers that twined the porch posts. Being inside her would bring deep satisfaction and a restfulness Mason hadn't known since ... well, he'd never known such things.

Mason was wildness, and Jasmine was peace. He spread his hand across her back and scooped her closer.

Jasmine abruptly jerked her head back, breaking the kiss, though she didn't try to pull from his embrace. "No. You're gorgeous and all, Mason, but I shouldn't do this."

Mason's skin was fever hot, his mouth not happy that the cool smoothness of her lips had gone. "Do what?" he asked, his voice hoarse.

"Take advantage of you." Jasmine touched a finger to his lips. "I'm upset, and I'm going for reassurance. That's not fair to you."

Not fair to *him*? What the hell was she talking about?

Jasmine put gentle hands on his arms and broke his hold. "I do this. I just want a little relief from loneliness, and I end up engaged to a total jerk and not coming to my senses until I'm addressing the wedding invitations."

Mason stared at her, the heat in his body far from assuaged.

"You seem like a nice guy," Jasmine went on, resting her fingers on his chest—which just showed she knew crap all about Shifters. None of them were *nice*. "I don't want to hurt you."

Now Mason wanted to laugh. He leaned to her, trapping her hand with his.

"Listen, sweetheart," he said in a hard voice, "if I'm kissing you, it's because I *want* to kiss you. Not because you're upset or alone, but because you're pretty in the twilight and I want to taste you. Has nothing to do with anything else, and you can't hurt me."

"I haven't hurt you *yet*," Jasmine said. "But I will when I tell you the wedding's off, or bury you under the floor in my house — or you'll break it off because you find a woman you want to be with who isn't a crazy psychic in a creepy old house."

Mason listened in bafflement then stopped her flow of words by touching her mouth. "I don't care about any of that. I came to have you help me find a Shifter healer, and now I'm going to fix your guitar. If we kiss along the way, then we do. All right?" He lifted himself from her, his heart pounding, the mating frenzy that lurked inside every Shifter flickering on the edges of his sanity. *The guitar,* he told himself. *Focus on the guitar.*

He blew out a breath and made himself turn away from Jasmine. "Now, let me look at this thing."

***

Jazz watched numbly as Mason laid out the broken pieces of the Martin, his blunt fingers gentle as he touched the wood.

His hands had been as gentle on Jazz's body. She still felt the imprint of them on her back.

Still felt the heat of his kiss too. Her knees had started to fold as she'd sagged against his chest. He was warmer than a human man, the fabric of his shirt and jacket holding all kinds of heat.

Mason shrugged the jacket off now, no longer worried about being exposed as a Shifter. Porch light slid down arms bared by his shirt and glinted on the silver and black Collar around his throat.

He bent over the guitar, fingers moving almost tenderly as he removed the strings and set them aside. "The neck's intact. That's good. Didn't get bent. I can save a lot of this, but I'll have to cut a few new pieces. It will look the same but I can't guarantee it will sound the same. It will still sound good," he added quickly as though thinking Jazz worried about that, "but its voice will be different." He said this regretfully, gazing at the guitar as he might a friend who was ill and broken.

"If you can fix it, that would be awesome," Jazz said. "Tell you what—you fix my guitar, I'll find your healer, and we'll call it even."

Mason's skeptical look returned. He'd dealt with her house without fear, not questioning that it had trapped and terrified Lucas on purpose, but he obviously didn't believe in Jazz's abilities at all.

Jazz went on when he didn't answer. "I'll prove it to you. I'll tell you everything there is to know about Mason McNaughton. If I'm wrong about any of it, I'll pay you whatever is fair for fixing the guitar and say good-bye, no hard feelings." She offered her hand. "Deal?"

Chapter Five

Mason stared at the hand Jazz stuck out as though not quite sure what to do with it. He looked into her eyes, his gray ones quiet, set down the last string, and closed his fingers over hers.

"Deal."

Jazz stopped herself from making any kind of noise as his aura engulfed her, the wildness of him coming through. It was as though she sought to befriend an untamed animal, pretending she wasn't afraid as she touched him. Mason held her with his gaze, stilling her.

She drew a quick breath and jerked her hand from his grasp.

"All right." Jazz waved him to sit while she rummaged in her shelves.

Mason turned back to the guitar as though not at all interested in what Jazz was doing, but she saw his eyes gleam in the rising moonlight as he watched her.

She set votive candles in holders on the veranda's railing and a few on the table, well away from the pieces of guitar, and lit them. Next she studied her tarot decks and picked the three she thought would work best.

Stones came next. Jazz liked working with stones and crystals, finding a connection with them. Not all psychics did—some preferred incense, wind chimes, or candles to assist them, but the stones enhanced Jazz's abilities. Plus, the colors and shapes were pleasing.

Mason flicked his gaze to them as she laid them out—obsidian, tiger's eye, amber, and a smoky quartz the color of his eyes. The candles flickered in a breath of breeze, then burned straight and tall.

"I didn't finish reading your hand," Jazz said. "But I'll do that later. I was right about the creative bend to the head line. It's very strong."

"Mmm," Mason said. He finally laid the pieces of guitar aside and turned to focus on what she was doing.

When he focused, he really did it. No halves. Mason's wolf stare fixed on her, the predator in him never far away. Jazz's blood tingled hot and she forced her attention to her task.

"I'm going to do several tarot readings on you," she said quickly. "A traditional one, and then I have readings that I've come up with myself. I find that several different types of readings are better to clear out any psychic blocks you might have put up, intentionally or unintentionally."

Mason only watched her—a wolf waiting for the rabbit to realize she was his next target.

Jazz thrust the first deck of cards at him, trying to stem her nervousness. "Here, shuffle those. When you're done, shuffle these as well." As Mason took the first deck, Jazz laid the other two in front of him.

Mason moved the cards between his fingers, pulling the pack apart and shoving it together again. The moonlight filtered through the leaves of the rose vines, making his eyes silver in the shadows.

He finished with the cards, slapped the pack down in front of her, and picked up the next one. While he shuffled, again with slow deliberation, Jazz smoothed out the silk cloth she'd laid on the table and adjusted the candles and crystals around it.

Mason finished with the second pack and picked up the third. Jazz waited until he had shuffled that one and set it back down with the same impatient thump.

"We'll start with the reason you came to see me." Jazz willed her fingers to still as she drew a card from the top of the first deck and turned it over. "Knight of Wands. Hmm, not too surprising."

Mason leaned forward, his brows drawing together. "Why? What's it mean?"

Jazz touched the card, which depicted a knight on horseback, who seemingly didn't notice he was holding a wand at his side. "The first card is all about you and why you're here—you came to me so I can help you find someone. The Knight of Wands can mean a journey—you're seeking something, but you don't have a specific direction to travel. It's also about you personally. You were restless and needed to leave home, seeking to do something about the situation—you don't trust anyone else to do it. You're brave but a little reckless." Jazz let herself smile. "As proved when you picked up Lucas like a sack of potatoes and carried him out of here. I'll have to thank you for that. I was trying to find a graceful way to break up that didn't involve a terrible fight."

Mason gave her a nod. "No problem."

Jazz caught a glimmer of humor in his voice, and she wondered what he'd said to Lucas before Lucas had driven off in a big hurry.

Jazz pulled her concentration back to the cards. "Let's find out how this quest will go ..." She turned over another card and laid it crosswise on top of the knight. "Oh," she said in some dismay.

"Oh?" Mason jerked his attention to her. "What *oh?*"

"This card is the Tower." Jazz indicated the picture of the tower that tumbled down, spilling bricks as it went. She continued quickly, trying to make her voice bright. "Which, can be, you know, a positive card if you put the right interpretation on it."

"I have no idea *what* it means," Mason growled. "You're saying I'm a knight, but I have to charge a tower that's already falling apart? This is total bullshit."

Jazz stopped her next words. She'd been speaking to him as she would a client at the store, people who wanted advice but didn't necessarily want bad news. The Tower could be taken to mean something like a breakthrough, but most often in her experience, it meant a negative force.

"It means your journey is going to be difficult," she confessed. "That you might not find what you seek."

"It's already difficult," Mason said in a hard voice. "Staying home was *more* difficult. I don't really care what I have to do to fix this."

He didn't. Jazz read anger in him, frustration, even some helplessness. This wasn't a man who liked these feelings, and he struggled with them. His aura told her that.

"Let's keep on," Jazz said, trying to sound soothing. She laid down the next card above the first two. "Ah, not bad. The Eight of Wands. This tells you to move forward, while you can—don't wait. The Tower indicates the way will be difficult, but the Eight of Wands shows that it's a great time for your quest."

"Does it?" The words were flat, not really a question. "What else?"

"Let's look at your past foundation," Jazz said as she turned over the next card. "Page of Wands— hmm, you're getting a lot of wands, another indication you need to continue your quest immediately. The page tells me that you've had a lot of support in the past, loyalty from those around you."

Mason huffed a breath. "Seriously? You've never been in a Shifter family have you? Try being the youngest of a bunch of pain-in-the-ass wolves. Alphas who like to remind you constantly that you're the bottom of the pack. Even the crazy feral thinks he out-dominates me. Or he would if he wasn't a crazy feral. My brothers are loyal only when they want something."

He spoke with conviction but Jazz read something in Mason's tone that contradicted his words. He wasn't lying—he meant everything he said—but there was more to his situation than he was letting on. Maybe he really did believe everyone treated him like he was the least important member of his family, but Jazz had difficulty imagining anyone dismissing him. Mason so dominated every inch of space around him that Jazz couldn't believe he didn't put everyone else in their place.

"Anyway," she said, and quickly laid the next card beneath the crossed cards. "Ah. The Magician. Thought so. It's very like you."

Mason studied the card. "I'm like a magician when I don't believe in magic?"

"You *do* believe in magic," Jazz countered. "You just don't believe in *me*." She gave him a smile, but his lack of trust stung a little. "The Magician card tells me you're someone who believes in taking action. You're also creative and resourceful, and will do whatever you can to finish what you need to. All of this ..." She waved her hand to indicate the turned-over cards ... "Influenced your decision to go on a quest no one else wanted to undertake."

"They didn't try very hard to stop me," Mason said, frowning. "I think they were just happy I shut up and left."

If that was true, then Jazz didn't think much of these Shifters that had sent him off. Mason at least had gotten off his ass and tried to help.

Jazz turned over the next card. "Strength," she said, pointing to it. "Again, not surprised. Your aura has a lot of strength. This is what's going to get you through this quest, is what's going to help you against the many obstacles the Tower says are coming." She touched the crossed cards. "All in all, this is a good reading so far. It's telling me that even though the way is going to be tough, everything about you will help you win in the end."

She sat back, pleased, ready to deal the final four cards and complete the reading.

Mason's strong hand on her wrist stopped her. "Enough of this. Can you help me find the guy or not?"

Jazz's heart beat faster, both in anger and at the hot streak of longing at his touch. "I might be able to if you let me finish," she said hastily. "It could tell us where to start looking."

Mason's grip didn't loosen. "They're *cards*. Pieces of cardboard someone printed at a factory. They don't mean *anything*." He let go of Jazz and swept his hand over the cloth, scattering cards every which way. "If you can't help me, I'll fix your guitar and then be on my way."

Jazz lost her temper. She'd been derided by people before who didn't believe in psychics and scoffed throughout readings. But Mason pissed her off. Just because he was hot, and yeah, she'd enjoyed the hell out of that kiss, didn't mean she was going to sit here and let him insult her. She was the best damn psychic in New Orleans. She had the true gift, and everyone who was anyone knew it.

"All right," she snapped. Jazz shoved the decks aside then reached out and cupped his face in her hands. "I'll tell you what I know. You're arrogant and full of yourself, though I don't have to be a psychic to know that. You're the youngest of your family, which means your brothers have always expected you to be naive and do a lot of the grunt work. Because of that, you've retreated into your craft to make yourself feel better and have some sense of control. You've perfected your craft so much that now your brothers envy you the skill but they don't often tell you so. You lost your mom not long ago, and it hurt you bad, but you haven't been able to talk about it to anyone. She died of grief because your father was killed tragically a while back ... Oh." Jazz trailed off and swallowed, her anger dying into shock. "He was shot. Oh, Mason, I'm so sorry."

Mason jerked from her. "None of this is a big secret. Bree could have told you all that."

Jazz shook her head, her heart squeezing in compassion. "She didn't. She told me your name and that you were a Shifter from Austin trying to find someone. I'm so, so sorry about your mom and dad."

She'd pieced together the entire story from his aura and the chilling anguish that nearly leapt out at her. But it didn't matter. He'd been through grief. Perhaps his brothers didn't even understand how much he'd been hurting.

Mason, she'd seen, had witnessed his dad's death. He'd been about nine, still a very young cub. That moment had changed him from a happy kid who was a little bit complacent to a stunned and lonely child, raw and hurting. He still smarted from it, Jazz could see. Jazz knew from her own experience that some people didn't think the very young had enough comprehension to feel profound grief and loss, bewilderment and emptiness, but they did.

Mason only looked at her. There was rage in him, though not necessarily for her.

Jazz put her hand on his, squeezing a little. "I'm sorry," she repeated, her voice soft.

Mason jerked, but he didn't pull away. His anger flared then it died, bit by bit, until it was a smoldering glow. He cleared his throat. "Thank you."

That *thank you* was hard for him. Mason wasn't used to compassion, she was coming to understand. Jazz had seen, when his past and present had rushed by her, that his brothers and aunt had gotten through their pain by not speaking of it. They'd stayed together, their closeness apparent, but his brothers weren't the kind of men who talked about their feelings.

They sat in silence for a time, while the moon rose higher, and a light breeze moved the rose vines. The air cooled the residual heat of the May day, a welcome relief.

They stayed there until Mason gently withdrew his hand and sat back. "The Shifter I'm looking for apparently doesn't like being found," he said, as though the secrets of his pain hadn't been revealed. "From what I understand, healers like to hide. I don't know if it's because they have to or because they're wussy."

Jazz tried a smile. "So we scour two countries for a wussy Shifter?"

Mason grunted what might have been a laugh. "For a Goddess-touched wussy Shifter."

"Goddess-touched?" Jazz lifted her brows. "Hmm. We might be able to use that. You're a little Goddess-touched yourself." Jazz reached out and brushed one finger across his cheek. "I saw it when I read you."

Mason stilled. His anger died all the way into cool ashes, but another kind of heat filled his gaze.

The bristles of his whiskers were rough on Jazz's fingertips. Moonlight sparkled in his eyes, which were again fixed on her, a flush on his face.

"There's Guardian ancestry in my family," Mason said quietly, deliberately sitting back to put himself out of her reach. "It's why a broken piece of sword talked to my brother, probably why I can understand your house. But I'm beat. I'll see what I can do with this in your shop then turn in. We'll look for Shifter healers in the morning."

He scraped back his chair and stood up, lifting the broken guitar.

Jazz gaped at him in surprise. A moment ago, he'd been impatient for her to put away the divining tools, look into the air, and pull out the name of the man, his exact address, and how to get to him. Now he looked down at her, waiting for her to show him the way to the shop.

Jazz rose quickly, unnerved by him standing over her. She'd have to go past him to fetch the keys from the table in the hall, and he stood like a barrier, his bulk filling the gazebo.

But he stepped back as Jazz ducked by with a quick, "Excuse me," making sure she didn't touch him at all. Jazz snatched up the keys from the drawer in the table, turned on the yard lights with switches inside the back door, and walked outside again.

Mason had already left the veranda via the back steps and waited for her on the path that led to the outbuildings. Jazz held out the keys, and Mason took them.

Jazz snatched her hand back and pointed into the darkness. "It's along this path and then to the left, behind another clump of trees. There are no lights down there until you get inside. If you wait a sec, I'll find you a flashlight."

Mason closed his hand around the keys with a *clank*. "Shifters can see in the dark." He started to turn away then he swung around again and took two steps forward, closing the small distance between them.

His eyes had gone Shifter white. They were sharp in the night, fixing on her with an intensity she'd never encountered before. Even the Shifter Jazz had gone out with years ago had never looked at her like this.

Mason abruptly snaked his arm around her waist, pulled her against him, and brought his mouth down on hers.

The kiss was hard, thorough. Jazz went rigid even as her body caught fire. She lost track of all sensation but his mouth on hers, his hand hard on her neck, the full length of his body, the press of his fingers on her skin. She wanted to stand in the darkness, her house lit behind her, and kiss him forever, his body solidly against hers, his strength holding her up.

Cold struck her as Mason pulled back, his breath touching her lips, making them tingle. He stared down at her for a few heartbeats, then as suddenly as he'd seized her, he released her.

Jazz staggered but caught herself as Mason stepped away.

"I wanted to kiss you *that* time too," he said in a low voice. He studied her a moment longer, then he turned around without a word and strode into the shadows, his boots crunching on the graveled path.

He faded from Jazz's sight between one step and the next. He was there, and then gone. A faint wolf snarl came out of the darkness, then she heard the shop door slam.

Jazz let out her breath, the sound loud in the darkness. Goddess defend her, he was a *damn* good kisser.

But he was Shifter, Jazz reminded herself. Shifters were compelling and drew you in before you could stop yourself. Later they broke your heart, and you ended up eating way too much ice cream, and drinking at Mardi Gras with your friends until you woke up with no memory of how you came to be in the back of a pickup missing your bra and one of your stockings. To this day, Jazz had no idea why only the one.

But Jazz couldn't deny, as she turned her steps to the house, that the late spring night was far colder and emptier without Mason in it.

***

Mason spent a long time standing in the middle of the workshop after he turned on its lights, growling and cursing.

Damn it, why did she have to be warm and arousing? Alluring and sensual? Why did she have dark blue eyes and a smile that lit up the world the few times she'd flashed it?

His brief taste of Jasmine hadn't been enough. Mason wanted to lace his fingers through her hair, finding every lock of brown among the black. He wanted to learn the satisfaction of sliding off her clothes, touching her skin, lifting the weight of her breasts while he kissed her. He wanted to discover whether her tattoo really did encircle her breast and then to follow its path with his tongue.

It had taken every bit of strength he'd had to walk away from her tonight. She'd told him she sensed strength in his aura, in the cards she'd turned over for him. Well, that strength was the only thing that had kept him from carrying her into the house and upstairs and nestling down with her.

He surprised himself. While Shifters instinctively craved sex, Mason hadn't had much experience with it yet. He'd never looked at a woman, especially a human one, and pictured being with her so vividly — in blood-pounding detail.

Didn't matter, though. Jasmine didn't like Shifters. She hadn't said that in so many words, but Mason could tell — her body language had shouted her discomfort with him as soon as he'd seen her standing on the porch. Jasmine had enjoyed the kisses but she'd taken the blame on herself for that first kiss, believing her own weakness had let her down.

There was nothing weak about her. Jasmine had then looked at Mason and told him all about himself. Sure, she could have learned much of his history from Bree or anyone in the Austin Shiftertown — everyone in a Shiftertown knew everyone else's business. But Jasmine had revealed things that Mason had never told anyone in his life.

He remembered the horrible day his father had died, when he'd gone from innocent cub to messed-up Shifter in one second. Jasmine had understood — he'd seen that in her. Woo-woo magic or not, she drew forth what Mason had felt and knew exactly what he'd gone through. She'd said she'd lost her parents as well, but it had been more than that.

Her compassion made Mason want to draw her to him, hold her in the night, wake to her in the morning. But if he walked into the house and up to her bedroom, she might become angry and take that compassion back. Her mistrust of Shifters might kick in, and Mason needed her help.

Plus, Mason knew he wouldn't be able to take it if Jasmine looked at him with the disgust groupies got when he suggested they go out somewhere and get to know each other, not just have quick sex in the parking lot. To groupies, Shifters carried the excitement of the forbidden. They weren't guys they actually wanted to *be* with.

Mason continued to snarl as he prepared himself for the night. He left the shop and went around the house to walk his motorcycle into the back, checking the place over for any danger as he did so. He parked it in front of the shop and removed his small duffel bag of clothes.

Inside the workshop again, he dropped the bag on the small bed in the corner then turned to the guitar.

Criminal. This Lucas guy was a total asshole. What kind of person would damage a guitar like this? A work of art?

Mason ground his teeth as he laid out the parts. The neck was in pretty good shape, but the body was a wreck. The rim was all right, which was good, but the bottom and top pieces would have to be replaced. Mason could do it, and it would be good as new, but never again have the personality of a fifty-year-old Martin.

He couldn't do much here, though. This was a decent shop — he looked with admiration at the lathe, belt sander, and several different types of scroll saws. But Mason needed his own place with its collection of exotic woods that he could plane to just the right thickness, and his hand tools he knew like old friends. And—he had to admit it—he wanted Broderick, who was a little more experienced than Mason and could give advice on how to put the guitar back together.

Mason found a couple of boxes and bubble wrap and started packing up the guitar—the body in one box, neck in another. He'd take the pieces back to Austin and fix the guitar after he found the healer.

Mason stripped off as he packed it up. It was hot here, no air flowing in the small shop, the bright lights not helping. Mason took everything off except his boxer-briefs, sweat dripping down his torso. He should have risked asking Jasmine to find him a room in the main house, where she might have air conditioning, or at least a big fan.

No, no, if he went to the house, Mason would want to climb the stairs, find Jasmine's bedroom, and snuggle in with her. He wondered if the house would let him do that. Would it simply throw him down the stairs? Or encourage him to stay with her?

Creepy place.

He must have been way too focused on the guitar and Jasmine, because he didn't hear the step until the door was already wide open. Mason hadn't locked it, not worried about any intruder he couldn't handle.

Until he looked into the enraged eyes of Lucas, Jasmine's now ex-boyfriend, and at the semiautomatic pistol he held. Mason had the presence of mind to shove the guitar to the back of the table and dive for the floor just as Lucas opened fire.

Chapter Six

Jasmine's psychic instincts alerted her to the intruder well before she heard the shots. She jolted out of a sound sleep, perspiring and hot from a very erotic dream that involved Mason, a bathtub, and a lot of scented oils, to hear silence.

Something was wrong. The house was tense, and Jasmine's body was coiled and rigid, her mind straining to pick out the real from the imagined.

Mason was out there alone in the wood shop, a relatively new building that had nothing to do with the house. The house's protection extended to the old kitchens and slave quarters and that was it. Anything built after 1920 was on its own.

Jazz scrambled out of bed, pulled on shorts, top, and sneakers, and hurried down the stairs. She'd reached the bottom when she heard the gunshots.

Mason.

She rushed down the hall, lifted the baseball bat she kept inside the cellar door, and ran out the back.

She'd lived in this part of Louisiana long enough to not dash outside and look around every time she heard gunfire—she'd learned to wait and see whether her neighbors were shooting at snakes or gators or each other. But Mason was out here, alone and vulnerable. She should have let him stay in the house, Jazz knew, but she hadn't trusted herself to keep away from him. Shifters were her kryptonite.

As she started down the veranda stairs, keeping to the shadows, a figure sprinted toward her from the direction of the wood shop. Jazz stared, her mouth open. Lucas.

Behind him came a huge wolf, a creature born of shadows and moonlight. He charged after Lucas, silver light brushing his gray fur and Shifter eyes.

Jazz backed up the stairs. Lucas, on the path, turned and fired wildly, completely missing the wolf. Bullets pinged into the ground, and deafening gunfire filled the air.

The wolf came on, sparks around his neck like a ring of fire. Lucas dashed for the veranda, not even noticing Jazz.

Jazz swung the baseball bat. It contacted, not with Lucas, but the gun, which went skittering across the porch. It went off as it fell, and Jazz screamed.

Lucas's eyes widened as he finally became aware of her standing there but he ran on into the house, not bothering to stop to pick up the gun. The wolf leapt after him, barreling through the back door on Lucas's heels. Jazz, clutching the bat, hurried after them.

Lucas was in the staircase hall, which had obligingly lit up when Jazz had run down from her bedroom. He was clutching a newel post, trapped in the hall by the wolf, who blocked the way out. Lucas gave the wolf a look of sheer panic then he turned and dashed up the stairs.

There was no doubt about the house's involvement this time. With a vast yawning sound, the staircase parted in the middle. Lucas fell, screaming, to the space between it, then the stairs rushed together, and the wooden steps closed with a snap.

Jazz and the wolf were left blinking at the staircase, which lay smooth and seamless before them as though nothing had happened.

Lucas wasn't dead, though. Jazz heard him shouting, his terrified cries muffled. There was a tiny room under the stairs—a hidden door behind the staircase that Jazz always kept locked, so a tourist wouldn't get stuck in there.

She turned to the wolf, who eyed her, growling, his nose wrinkling with his snarl. He was a beautiful animal, the darker gray fur on his back swirling to light gray across his broad chest. A black V pointed down his forehead and faded out on his nose.

From this face, hard eyes fixed on Jazz and didn't release her. The Collar had stopped sparking, but it was obvious on his neck, encircling his throat. Jazz's Shifter ex-boyfriend had told her that Fae magic ensured the Collar expanded and contracted as they shifted.

"Mason?" Jazz said, taking a tighter grip on the bat. "Is that you? Nice wolfie."

The expression on the wolf's face turned to one of annoyance. He shook himself, a doglike movement, then the wolf began to distort and change.

The fur receded, smooth human skin taking its place at the same time claws and paws changed to hands and feet. Mason rose as his hind legs became human, his front legs, muscular arms. His nose shrank until the wolf face was Mason's handsome one, touched with dark whiskers.

His eyes changed last. They remained focused on Jazz, the very light gray slowly darkening to the raincloud gray of Mason in human form.

"Wolfie?" he asked with a Shifter snarl.

Only the voice and his eyes reminded Jazz he was animal inside. The rest of him was pure human male. Naked and hard-bodied, in her hallway.

Whatever clothes he'd worn were gone. Mason was bare and unashamed, resting his hands on his hips as he caught his breath.

"You okay?" he asked her. His gaze moved pointedly to the baseball bat, which she still hefted.

"Yeah, I—" Jazz broke off as she caught sight of what Mason's shifting body had distracted her from seeing. He had blood all over his shoulder, as well as smeared down his arm and side. "Are *you* all right?" She dropped the bat with a clatter and hurried forward. "Did he get you?"

"Grazed me," Mason said without worry as Jazz reached him. "I'll be fine. Shifters heal fast."

So he said, but at the same time, he swayed. Jazz put her hand on his arm and found his skin hot and damp.

"You're not all right," she said with conviction. "You sit down."

Mason turned away from her and headed to the back hall. "I'll get over it. I just need a little rest."

Jazz watched him go, her mouth open, the view of his tight back and smooth backside well worth looking at.

But he was going to walk away, back to bed, like nothing had happened. *I was shot and your house ate your boyfriend, but oh well. Time for some shuteye.*

Jazz went out right after him. She had to run, and only caught up to him when he was halfway to the shop. Mason could *move.*

"You're not all right," Jazz repeated. "What's going on? Is there a bullet still in you?"

Mason turned and looked down at her. Under the filter of the trees, the moonlight made his skin variegated, dark and light. "My Collar went off," he said. "It makes me sick. But like I said, I'll get over it."

Jazz stepped to him in concern and put her hand on his forearm. His skin was already cooler, but clammy. "I know you're all-powerful and mighty, but you lost blood and were shocked. You need to stop."

Mason's gaze lowered, his body stilling. He took a long breath, chest rising, his lashes brushing his cheeks as he focused on her hand.

Jazz felt his pulse, strong and steady but rapid. The skin of his wrist was cool, the wiry hair on his forearm catching her fingertips. Dark hair brushed his chest as well, another arrow of it below his navel leading to shadow.

Jazz lightened her touch, giving Mason's arm a soft stroke. Again, she couldn't stop herself. She for some reason wanted to be near him, in his warmth. Personal space had gone out the window.

Mason's fingers latched over hers. He carefully lifted her hand away, flicking his gaze to her face.

Jazz pulled back, self-conscious. "Sorry," she said. "I told you, I can't be trusted. I throw myself at a guy, and the next thing I know, he's shooting people in my house or running off with another Shifter he swore up and down he'd never noticed before, leaving me in broken little pieces."

Mason's brows drew down, and Jazz snapped her mouth shut. She hadn't meant to tell him that.

He continued to frown at her, as though trying to figure out what she was all about. Then he jerked his head up and swung around to scan the darkness.

Jazz came alert too, her psychic shields once again indicating danger.

"Cops," Mason said. He cocked his head, listening hard. Jazz heard nothing, but Shifter hearing was superior to a human's.

Mason was already turning away, moving swiftly to the wood shop. By the time Jazz made it in behind him, he had donned a pair of underwear and was reaching for his jeans and shirt. Jazz got a nice view of his backside cupped by tight boxers before he pulled up and zipped the jeans and jerked the shirt down his torso.

He shrugged on his jacket, covering his Collar once more, then grabbed the duffel and two wooden boxes.

He was leaving. Mason moved past Jazz and out the door. She leaned against the doorframe, watching as he shoved the duffel and boxes into his motorcycle's saddlebags.

Of course he was leaving. Either Lucas had called the cops on Mason before he'd come, or the neighbors had heard the gunfire and called the police. Jazz's neighbors were trigger-happy themselves, but they'd have been alarmed to hear shots at *her* house and want to make sure she was all right.

Jazz could now hear the sirens on the wind. The police would find Lucas penned in her house, he'd babble an incoherent and terrified story, and Mason would be blamed. Mason was Shifter. He'd be taken in, and probably terminated. That's what happened to Shifters who harmed humans.

Mason straightened up after securing the saddlebags and looked straight at her.

"Come with me," he said.

Jazz blinked. "What?"

"Come with me." His voice was low, rapid, rough. "Lucas will blame you and your crazy house. And me. And I still need your help."

Jazz continued to stare at him. "But, I—" The word *can't* died on her lips.

There were a million reasons she shouldn't go with him. *I can't leave my house. I can't leave my job and my clients. I can't just up and run away with a Shifter I met today because he has pretty eyes and a gorgeous body.*

The sirens grew louder. Yep, definitely heading this way.

Her heart fluttered. Jazz had lived most of her life in this house, on this quiet road along the river. Industry had encroached it, and the beauty of the land had been marred, but it was all she knew. That and driving the road into New Orleans every day, to friends, crowds, tourists, her life.

As many times as she advised her clients to follow their adventurous streak and try new things, Jazz never did.

The house behind her meant safety, comfort. Mason, the unknown. Danger. Uncertainty.

She didn't have time to draw a tarot card or cast a rune to tell her what to do. For the first time in her life, Jazz had to rely on her own judgment.

Jazz sucked in a breath, slightly dizzy. She was crazy, but she felt a sudden freedom blossoming inside her, looming up through her chest and lightening every part of her. She felt herself floating, giddy, wanting to laugh.

"What the hell?" she said breathlessly. "All right, yes. I'll come with you."

Mason's eyes flickered. Whether he was pleased with her decision or not, she couldn't tell. He simply turned to the bike.

"Wait," Jazz said. "I need my supplies. From the gazebo—in the big velvet bag."

Mason studied her a moment without blinking then he turned and made for the veranda. He moved so swiftly Jazz lost him a few times in the shadows, then found him again, a man running with lithe, athletic grace.

Within seconds, Mason was back, carrying her bag that held cards, stones, herbs, and other things she'd need to do divination. "This it?"

When Jazz nodded, he quickly stowed her accoutrements in his saddlebag then straddled the bike and reached for the starter. "Come on. Is there a back road out of here?"

Jazz hesitated one more moment, folding her arms, hugging herself. Behind her lay the protection of her grandmother's house, enclosing walls that would never let anything bad happen to her. Before her, Mason, a Shifter she barely knew, and the open road. Darkness, insecurity.

Oh, for crap's sake. If I don't leave now, I never, ever will.

Mason watched her impatiently. If she hesitated too long, he'd have no choice but to ride away. He had to go before the police found him and dragged him off to a cage.

Jazz flung her arms open, as though releasing herself to the wind. She launched herself at the bike and scrambled up onto the seat behind him, using Mason's body to steady herself.

Mason already had the motorcycle going, the large machine rumbling beneath her. Jazz wrapped her arms around Mason, balancing herself as her biker ex-fiancé had taught her years ago. Mason eased the motorcycle forward and pulled carefully onto the back lane Jazz directed him to, moving slowly to not make too much noise.

Police cars poured down the front drive of the old house, sirens blaring, lights flashing red in the night. Jazz and Mason quietly slid out the back way, Jazz heading into her future with her eyes shut tight.

***

Mason drove north. He figured that by the time the police freed Lucas — if the house let them — and got a coherent story from him, they'd start searching for them east into New Orleans, or west toward the giant city of Houston. Mason instead rode straight north, out of bayou country and away from the river.

He drove for hours, heading north and west to Shreveport and then west across the border into

Texas. Once in Texas he'd at least not be automatically arrested for being a Shifter out of his state, even if the police questioned why he was out on a back highway with a beautiful woman in the middle of the night.

Jasmine was hanging on to him, the warmth of her against his back erasing the pain of his injury and Collar shock. Mason was usually hungover for a while after his Collar went off, but with Jasmine holding him, the queasiness had faded much faster than usual. Likewise, any ache from the bullet that had grazed him was gone.

Mason could have kept riding through the early hours of the morning, turning the bike south to head for Austin, but Jasmine was exhausted. He'd given her his jacket early into the trip, knowing she wasn't used to having her bare skin buffeted by the wind. The night was dark enough not to expose his Collar, and the cool wake of the moving bike felt good to him.

He'd not seen a cop on the road, other than ones making their leisurely way along without lights or sirens, or manning speed traps that Mason made sure not to spring. Either the police were looking in the wrong place for them, or they'd taken Lucas's story of wolves and staircases swallowing him as crazed ravings.

On the far side of a dark Texas town, Mason pulled into the parking lot of a one-story motel. It was about three in the morning, and the motel's office was locked up and dark.

Mason parked the bike and knocked on the office's door, but no one answered. Probably the manager had gone home or was asleep, this place too quiet to get much business.

Only a few vehicles lingered in front of the tiny motel. Mason signaled for Jasmine to wait at the motorcycle as he moved past the doors, listening and testing the air for scents to determine which rooms were empty.

When he reached the last room, he waved Jasmine over. She'd already climbed off the bike, and she surreptitiously rubbed her backside as she joined him at the door.

Mason touched the lock, which was a regular one that needed a key. "I can break this," he said, "but I'd rather be able to lock it again. A flimsy chain is only so good."

Jasmine's fingers landed on his shoulder. "That's all right. Let me. Can you grab my bag, please?"

Mason grunted, returned to the motorcycle, and pushed it over to the door. He fished the velvet carryall from his saddlebag, wondering what she needed from it.

Jasmine opened the bag's drawstrings and rummaged around in it. The light above the door shone into the bag, revealing all kinds of things— cards, stones, pouches, books … Mason had never figured out how women stuffed so much into their bags and purses. Women's purses had to be like the time machine on that British sci-fi show—bigger on the inside.

Jasmine pulled out a stick of incense and then a lighter. She lit the end of the stick, puffed on it gently until it glowed, then blew a tiny stream of smoke into the lock. She whispered a word Mason didn't know, and went motionless, waiting.

Nothing happened for a moment or two. Just as Mason was about to return to the suggestion that he break open the door, he heard a distinct *click*. Jasmine smiled, ground out the burning tip of the incense on the cement doorstep, and turned the knob.

Mason caught her by the arm before she could charge inside. Jasmine gave him a startled look, as had the women at Inspirations when he'd pushed in past them, but he stood her aside and walked into the room, scanning for danger.

He glanced into the bathroom, but his nose had already told him the room had been empty for some time. Once he determined all was well, he turned on the light and motioned Jasmine in behind him. She closed the door and looked around, rubbing her arms in his jacket sleeves. Her gaze fixed on the bed — there was only one.

"It's a Shifter thing, isn't it?" she asked, halting in the middle of the room. "Going first into a building and checking it out?"

"Yep." Mason dumped the duffel and her velvet bag to the table then locked and chained the door. "It's a Shifter thing. How'd you do that, by the way? Open the lock?"

Jasmine shrugged, her hands tight against her sides. "My grandmother taught me. It's a fairly basic spell."

"I thought you were psychic, not a witch," Mason said, opening his duffel bag. They'd have to buy her a toothbrush and other amenities in the morning.

"The gift is the gift, no matter what you call it," Jasmine said, her voice weak. "The problem is, it's air magic, and I'm best with earth magic. Any other kind wipes me out. There's only one bed."

She swayed as she made the last declaration, then her knees buckled and she collapsed.

Mason was there to catch her. He lifted Jasmine into his arms, her warmth and flowerlike scent undiminished from their long ride.

Jasmine looked up at him through half-closed eyes, tried to struggle, and gave up. "There's only one bed," she repeated, the words a mumble.

"I know," Mason said.

Chapter Seven

Jazz woke to sunlight streaming through badly fitted blinds into her face. She blinked open her eyes, wondering what had happened to her nice, soft bed, and then realized she wasn't in her own bedroom.

She lay face up beneath a sheet on a hard bed under a water-stained ceiling. At several points in its life, the roof had leaked.

The bed sagged heavily on her left, and Jazz turned her head that way.

Mason lay on his back on top of the sheet, his arm over his face, wearing nothing but a T-shirt and tight-fitting boxer-briefs. His chest rose and fell in sonorous breathing, and a light snore eased from his mouth.

Jazz carefully rose on her elbow to look at him. Mason was a big man, taking up a good portion of the supposedly king-sized bed. His body was trim and tight, in spite of his size, hard even relaxed in sleep.

He'd been a beautiful wolf, but he was beautiful in this form too. Jazz let her gaze run from his face, brushed by the sunlight that had awakened her, to the Celtic cross that lay against his throat.

The Collar kept Shifters tame, so humans claimed. Jazz had never quite believed that.

Here she was, on a bed with a man who was supposed to be a wild beast, crazed and out of control, theoretically subdued only by the Collar around his neck.

But she'd read Mason—his aura, his past. This wild beast loved, laughed, grieved. He'd been protective of Jazz from the moment he met her, he spoke of his brothers with gruff exasperation, and he loved his aunt. He'd touched the guitar with skilled and gentle fingers, and listened to Jazz try to play with interest, not derision.

If all wild things were like Mason, they wouldn't be so feared.

Then again …

She became aware of a pair of gray eyes on her, Mason's arm having come down while Jazz moved her scrutiny to his hard abdomen and very tight underwear.

"Hey," Mason grunted as she flushed. "You okay?"

Jazz tugged the sheet higher on her chest, though she wore the shirt and shorts she'd put on last night. "Just hungry. Where are we, anyway?"

Mason shrugged, the bed moving with his strength. "Hell if I know." He scanned the room as though that would give him some clue, then lay back down. "We'll rest here a while. You need it. Then we'll head to Austin."

"Austin?" she asked in surprise. "Why? I thought you were looking for your healer."

Mason rolled off the bed and came to his feet. "I know a house there where you can stay while we figure out how to find him. A house that doesn't eat people," he added as he turned away.

Mason standing up, his back to the bed, wasn't a bad view at all. The gray underwear hugged his ass, and his back held strength.

Unaware of her perusal, Mason stretched, giving a yawn worthy of his wolf. "I'll shower and go round up something to eat."

Jazz sat up to watch him stroll across the room and pause to grab clothes from his duffel. "Shouldn't I go for the food?" she asked. "You're Shifter. You might scare people, and then we'll have to run again."

Mason swung back to her, balling his clothes in his hands, scowl in place. "You're not going *anywhere* by yourself. You're probably the tastiest thing for miles around, and the Goddess knows who is out there to catch you."

Jazz blinked at him. His protectiveness had returned, stronger than ever.

"Wow," Jazz said, trying for a light tone. "I don't think anyone's called me *tasty* before."

"Then they're idiots," Mason said. "You stay here while I'm in the shower and don't go anywhere."

Jazz lifted her hands. "Don't worry. I don't know how to ride your motorcycle anyway. I'm only good at hanging on the back."

Mason watched her a moment longer, as though expecting her to bolt outside the second his back was turned. Finally, he swung around and stalked into the bathroom.

"Tasty," Jazz repeated. "I like that."

Mason shut the door, his frowning face and nice body disappearing from sight.

***

Mason wouldn't leave for food until Jazz had finished with the shower she wanted to take, then he instructed her to lock up behind him and not let *anyone* in but him.

Jazz felt a frisson of worry as Mason started the motorcycle and headed out—for Mason. Sure, he'd left her in a motel room in the middle of nowhere by herself with no transportation, but Jazz unfortunately did not have a lot of fear in strange situations—unfortunate, because it sometimes got her into trouble.

She was plenty resourceful. There was a land line here, and she could call friends back in New Orleans to come and get her—once she figured out where she was. She could also communicate with a few of her friends via scrying in water, though that wasn't always reliable. Water magic exhausted her even more than air magic.

One summer when she'd been in high school, Jazz and her grandmother had driven a beat-up RV all over the South, giving card and aura readings in small towns along the way. They'd made some money and had met amazing people. Jazz could always do that again, maybe finding another psychic in or near this little town with transportation.

Everything in life is an opportunity, her grandmother used to say. *Disadvantages can be turned into advantages. Just look around and count the possibilities.*

Jazz wasn't sure what possibilities were here yet, but she felt a pang as she remembered her grandmother's voice. She missed her.

Mason returned in a short time, without mishap, carrying fast-food breakfast. Jazz fell upon it hungrily, not worrying about things like grease, fat, and salt.

Mason ate carefully and slowly, not how she imagined a wolf would eat at all. Jazz tried to be sedate, but it had been many hours since she last had food, and she was *hungry.*

Once they finished, Mason gathered up all the trash and took it outside to throw it away. Jazz wiped off the table with one of the thin towels from the bathroom, and she opened her velvet bag as he came back in.

"Might as well get started," she said. "Can you tell me *anything* about this healer?"

Mason sat heavily in the chair on the other side of the table as Jazz drew out her rune stones, gathering them into her hand. "Nothing I haven't already told you."

"Right then." Jazz drew a breath and concentrated. "Healer. Has Goddess magic in him. Might be somewhere in two countries. Maybe."

Mason only gave her a nod, a glint of wry humor in him.

Jazz tried to picture what a Shifter healer might look like, but nothing came to her. She imagined a man with a Collar and a fuzzy aura around him, and tumbled the rune stones onto her cloth.

"Hmm," she said.

Mason rested his hands on the table's edge and leaned forward. "What?"

"It's a jumble." Jazz indicated the stones that had fallen every which way. "The runes for disruption and a stoppage are the most prominent. Blocking me."

She returned the stones to their drawstring bag, shook it, and held it out to Mason. "Draw a stone."

Mason's brows pinched together as he snaked his fingers into the bag and withdrew an amethyst. He turned it around so Jazz could read the symbol that looked like a lowercase letter T.

"Great." Jazz wrinkled her nose. "Means constraint, or again, a blocking. Either the universe is messing with me, or this healer doesn't want to be found. Putting up metaphysical blocking is like setting your cell phone to 'Do Not Disturb—Ever'."

Mason dropped the stone back into the bag. "How would he know we're looking for him? I didn't exactly tell the world. Only the Shifters who needed to know. And if *they* knew how to find him to warn him—then I wouldn't be looking for him. I'd just make them tell me where he was."

Jazz pictured Mason lining up the Shifters and glaring at them until they caved in with the knowledge. She said, "If this Shifter has the Goddess magic you say, he could easily set up wards to keep people from finding his location. Or he might not even know he's doing it."

Mason set the bag down with a click of stones and folded his arms. "How do you get through the blocks? Or—how about we stop with the magic shit and actually try to find him?"

Jazz gave him an irritated look. "Hey, do I question your ability to find things by scent? It's weird to me to watch you sniffing and then figuring out what's what from it. Well, this is *my* way of scenting." She leaned toward him, her hands on the table. "I can find him like this, Mason. I just have to keep trying."

Mason grunted low in his throat. "Whatever. If it doesn't work, I'm no worse off than I was before."

"It will work." Jazz took up the bag of runes, closed her eyes, and drew one. *Disruption.* Figures. "Just means I have to work a little harder, that's all."

She returned her runes to the large bag and opened her small box of stones. The aura of each stone came to her as she picked it up — the soothing fire of turquoise, the energy of the tiger's eye, the wisdom of ancient amber.

"What are you going to do with those?" Mason asked, sounding more curious than skeptical.

"They will help me open myself to the universe." Jazz placed each stone on her cloth, forming them into a semicircle with herself in the middle. "As I mentioned, I work best with earth magic. The stones — elements and compounds of the earth itself — will help me focus. These very stones have existed for ages, long before any of us got here. And here they are, continuing." She waved at the blue, yellow-gold, and black pieces glittering in the sunlight. "They'll continue after we're gone. If anything can help get me through a magical block, it's the bones of the earth."

Mason didn't answer. He fell silent as Jazz touched each stone, imbibing its strength. He went so still that she barely noted him breathing, and when he spoke again, she jumped.

"You were almost mated?" he asked. "You mentioned that you were addressing wedding invitations."

Jazz flushed as she moved her fingers to the Apache tear — the obsidian that was translucent black glass. She remembered babbling to him last night about her bad choices. "Yep. I was twenty. I'd met a guy when I was going to college in New Orleans and fell madly in lust with him. I thought it was true love. He was a biker, and I knew he had the reputation of being a bad boy, but that only made me want him more. I couldn't believe my luck when he asked me to marry him. He said he'd leave all the arrangements to me — whatever I wanted — and then show up at the church and we'd be together forever. Just the right thing to touch my romantic soul."

Mason's fingers had gone tight, his eyes lighter gray. "So, what happened? You finally saw through his bullshit?"

"I did. I was doing a mirror divination about our life together, and there he was. With one of my bridesmaids, both of them naked in her bed. He was saying how much fun they'd have when he got his hands on my grandmother's house and money." Jazz touched an amethyst, soothing the sting the memory brought. "I think the house helped me figure that out. I was using an antique mirror in my grandmother's boudoir — I'd never seen anything that clearly in a mirror divination before." She broke off with a little laugh, but that vision had hurt. Damn, had it hurt.

"Dick-wad," Mason growled. "When a man claims a mate, he doesn't betray that mate. Doesn't matter how many females wag their tails at him. And mating for treasure, that's just ... stupid. You were wise to dump him."

Jazz started to warm at his indignation but stopped herself. "You're sweet to say so, but don't tell me Shifters don't cheat." Another sting filled her heart, and she picked up the amethyst and squeezed it. "I dated a Shifter for a while. I know what happens."

Mason didn't move, didn't even stiffen, but Jazz sensed him come alert. "What Shifter? What are you talking about?"

"A Feline." More hurt welled up from Jazz's past to nestle in her heart. Dale had not been as muscular as Mason, but just as lithe—a mountain lion Shifter with tawny eyes. "He was from the New Orleans Shiftertown. I thought I'd give my friend Bree's suggestion a try and hang out at a Shifter bar. He was great, I thought." Dale had been a little bit wild, unpredictable, protective, like Mason. "But it turns out he was just another bad boy. I must have the gift for finding them. We were having a wonderful time, when one day he comes to me and says he's formed a mate bond—whatever that means—and he can't see me anymore. That's it. Done. Out of the blue. Next thing I know, he's mated with this Feline woman he'd sworn to me he didn't even like. He's been with her about seven years now, and they have kids. Cubs, I guess you'd say."

Jazz slammed down the amethyst as she finished then silently apologized to it. It wasn't the amethyst's fault. In fact, it was doing its best to make her feel better.

Mason didn't look as angry at this story. "When the mate bond forms, there's nothing a Shifter can do about it." He sounded less condemning, almost understanding. "It's a mystical bond that binds one Shifter with another. You have to be with that person, no matter what. It's physical pain if you're not."

Jazz tried to calm her temper. "How do you know? Have you formed this mate bond?" That would be just Jazz's luck—no, her *skill* at hungering after the wrong guy every time.

"My parents had the mate bond," Mason said quietly. "When my father was shot ..." He trailed off, his voice cracking. He cleared his throat. "My mother died that day. Not in body—she lived another twenty years. But there was nothing inside her. No hope, no joy, no life. Some Shifters can recover from a severed mate bond and form it again with another. But it's hard. The grief runs deep."

"Oh." Now Jazz felt like a fool. She'd banged on about how Dale had personally offended her, while Mason had watched his mother suffer because of this mate bond. "Damn. Mason, I'm so sorry." She reached across the table to his hand. "I bury myself in the metaphysical so much that I sometimes forget about real people and real life. But that's no excuse for me being stupid."

Mason jerked his brows together, his fingers clamping down on hers. "And if you rag on yourself one more time, I'm going to ..."

Jazz stopped. His grip was powerful, the bite of his fingers warm. "You're going to what?" she asked, pulse speeding, the space between her legs warming.

"I don't know," Mason said softly. "But it's going to be rough."

Jazz almost said, *Promise?* But she forced her mouth closed. Her attraction to dangerous men would get her into serious trouble one day. Look at her now, far from home, in a seedy motel with Mason, a Shifter who was barely tame. Did Jazz feel worry, fear, like a rational person should?

No, what coursed through her veins at the moment was pure excitement.

She yanked her hand from Mason's and started fumbling with the stones again, trying to steady herself.

"What about Lucas?" Mason asked. "Why him?"

"Lucas? I don't know, actually." The obsidian Jazz straightened was smooth, cool, absorbing her agitation. "He was good-looking, I was lonely ... I just kind of went along with it without thinking. That's easy to do, suddenly be in a relationship without bothering to stop and decide what you're doing. Then you realize he's mean and petty and your friends think you're a fool. The house didn't like him, which should have alerted me right away." Jazz sighed, wondering why she was babbling all this. But it was easy to talk to Mason's silence, his watchful stare.

Mason frowned. "Don't go out with anyone again who doesn't take care of you, Jasmine. You need someone who values you for who you are."

Right, as though guys like that were thick on the ground. "Easy for you to say," Jazz said irritably. All these healing stones around her, and she was tense and snappish. "You're gorgeous. I bet women fall all over themselves trying to be with you."

Mason's eyes flickered. "Only because they want to sleep with a Shifter."

Jazz heard the bitterness in his voice. He didn't continue, didn't elaborate. Enough said.

"Well, they don't know what they're missing," Jazz said hotly. "Any woman would be lucky to have you."

Another flicker. Jazz wondered how many women had told him that, right before they ran back home to their safe, non-Shifter parts of town. For them, being with Mason was a walk on the wild side, a taste of danger. Not a permanent thing. Jazz had heard plenty of women at Shifter bars express this sentiment. After all, he was a *Shifter*.

"I'm sorry," Jazz said, softening her tone. "I'm not mouthing words to make you feel better, I promise. Whoever you have the mate bond with will be truly lucky. I believe that."

A wordless growl came from Mason's throat. "If I don't find the healer, I might not live to *form* a mate bond."

Jazz lifted her hands. "I know. I know. I'm trying. Locating isn't an instant thing, especially when the person doesn't want to be found."

"You've found people before," Mason pointed out. "How did you do it then?"

Jazz stopped fussing with the stones and removed a small bronze bowl from her bag along with a sage smudge stick. "When I search for someone, I ask for an item special to them that I can hold to get a feel for their aura. In the case of the little girl, it was a stuffed dog she loved. I went to the top of my house and used that to track her aura, with the help of a lot of candles and crystals. Like tracing a radio signal back to its source. I found her fairly quickly. Turned out her oldest stepbrother had kidnapped her to ransom her off to her mother. He was a piece of work." She grimaced, remembering the young man's dark aura, his arrogance.

"She was found hidden at her stepbrother's apartment," Jazz went on. "Her stepbrother was arrested, and the little girl went home to her mom. For the man I looked for, it wasn't such a happy ending. He'd already been killed before the police even started the search. I at least could tell them where his body was." Jazz sighed. "Then the cops suspected *me* of having something to do with his death, because I found him when no one else could. Fortunately, I was able to prove I'd never heard of the guy before, never seen him, never been near him. But that's what happens. People don't believe in my gift. They think it's a trick."

Mason said nothing. He'd more or less accused her of the same thing, but he only acknowledged her jab with a level stare.

Jazz cleared her throat. "My point is it would be easier to find this healer if I had something of his. But I'll do my best."

Mason gave her a nod. "Thanks."

The flash of true gratitude heated Jazz until she flushed. The smoke from the sage she'd lit curled in her nose, and she coughed. She gave Mason a grin, waved the smoke away, and carried on.

***

Jasmine tried all day to find the healer. She stared into crystals, she waved smoke over them, she had Mason find her maps and she strewed crystal salt across them, bending down to read the swirls. She covered the table with her crystals, cards, candles, and little bells, even a bowl of water, saying she might as well throw everything together — air, earth, fire, and water. She consulted books and notes, jotted down words and runes, drew diagrams that Mason couldn't follow.

At one point she told him she'd do much better if he didn't sit there and watch her perform. Mason let out an annoyed breath but heaved himself up and out of the room.

He didn't tell Jasmine that it was a pleasure to watch her wave her hands gracefully over the smoke and stones, the flowers and vines on her arm moving in sinuous rhythm. How he liked listening to her low voice as she chanted, studying her face as her eyes closed, her lashes curling against her skin.

Mason could sit and watch her all day. He enjoyed remaining still and observing beauty.

He understood that he made her nervous though, so Mason left her alone — as alone as he would leave her. He hid his Collar under his jacket and went to the front office, where he paid for the night they'd already stayed and for the next one. The manager, a small man half Mason's size, didn't seem worried he'd broken into the room to sleep in it, though a little surprised Mason was bothering to pay. Mason settled up then went out and bought more food.

Jasmine ate in silence when he returned, discouraged. Mason didn't admonish her, only let her get back to what she was doing.

He napped later that afternoon, but Jasmine didn't stop or take a break. She was going to wear herself out, Mason thought when he woke to see her still hunched over her table. She was exhausting herself with woo-woo metaphysical stuff Mason didn't believe in, in an effort to help him.

What kind of woman did that?

Whoever you have the mate bond with will be truly lucky, Jasmine had said with that little smile on her face, her voice full of sincerity.

Mason had wanted to say the same right back to her. At the same time his wolf goaded him to find the men who'd hurt her and rip them to pieces — including the Shifter Feline, whoever he was. He noticed she carefully hadn't said his name.

Dirtbag should have explained to her about the mate bond from the start. It could form from nothing, would sink its claws in and not let go. At that point a Shifter had to follow the mate bond, no matter who he had to hurt to do it. Jasmine's Shifter should have told her of that possibility before the relationship had gone very far. Groupies knew about it, but Mason could tell that Jasmine was naive about Shifters.

But then, the guy was a *Feline*. Effing cats always thought they were better than anyone else. Bastards. They washed their faces with their own spit, for crap's sake.

"Oh!"

Jasmine sat up suddenly, her cry filling the room. She was staring into smoke rising from her bowl of sage, candles dancing, the light catching on the winking stones, as well as the bowl of water at her elbow.

Mason surged off the bed and moved to stand behind her. "What?"

"In the smoke." Jasmine pointed. "He's there. I see him. Right there. *Look!*"

Chapter Eight

Jasmine's unwavering finger pointed into the thin curtain of smoke rising from the sage.

Mason leaned over her shoulder to look. He wanted to sneeze, but he held it in as he peered where she pointed.

He saw only sage smoke, the flickering flames of candles behind it, a glitter of quartz and colored stones, and the dark blue velvet cloth it all rested on. Mason was about to straighten up and say he didn't see anything, when the smoke went suddenly opaque.

The flat gray obscured what he'd spied through it a second ago, and in the middle of the smoke, Mason saw a pair of eyes. They were black and fierce, and the rage behind them penetrated all the way into the room with Mason and Jasmine.

The eyes were set in a man's hard face, which was framed with two thin braids of pure white hair. The man's mouth and chin were dusted with a goatee beard as dark as his eyes. Those eyes met Mason's, the fury in them unmistakable.

He was a Shifter, Mason knew even through the fog. The man had the look, the bearing, the hard-ass manner, though Mason couldn't identify what kind of Shifter he was.

Mason also saw that he wasn't wearing a Collar.

The man snarled. He reached out a huge hand and batted the smoke away.

The smoke parted as though a puff of wind had torn it, and the image vanished. Mason and Jasmine were left staring at the remains of the sage, candlelight, and a scattering of stones.

Jasmine sat for one stunned instant, then she grabbed a map, upended the bowl, and dumped the smoldering sage right onto it.

Mason yelped as the map caught fire. He dove to grab it, but Jasmine threw herself into him and stopped him.

As they watched, a trickle of fire raced across the map and off its edge, forming a line heading rapidly northwest. The flame dragged the map completely to the carpet, where it began to smolder.

Mason shook off Jasmine's hold, leapt to the flames, and stomped on them until they died. The smoke from the fire rose in a single black streak that split in two—one half flowed back into the bowl, and the other surrounded Jasmine as though hugging her.

Jasmine was smiling broadly. She pressed her hands to her flushed face as the smoke dispersed. "You saw him, right?"

Mason nodded. "Yeah, I saw him. But the map burned up before it gave us a location."

"Doesn't matter." Jasmine beamed at him. "I know a direction. He's not in the continental United States. That line was moving northwest like a homing beacon. So he's in northwestern Canada or Alaska."

She looked so happy, so pleased, so beautiful with her eyes wide with joy. Mason couldn't stop himself going to her, catching her in his arms, and kissing her mouth.

Jasmine kissed him back readily, celebrating their breakthrough. She wound her arms around him, pulling him closer, smiling against his mouth.

Mason held her against him and deepened the kiss, and as he did, something changed in both of them. A spark lit Mason's blood, and under him Jasmine's body softened, flowing into his, need making her supple.

Mason slid his hands around her waist and up under her loose shirt to the smooth skin of her back. The top was one of the wispy things women liked to wear—layers serving in place of a bra and ties holding everything together. Mason began unraveling the ties, the thin fabric going slack.

Jasmine didn't fight him. She scooped herself closer to him, her arms tightening around his neck to draw him down to her.

Mason liked every curve of her, from the round of her hips, to her waist drawing in under the firm weight of her breasts. He caught one breast in his hand, the shirt giving enough to let him, enjoying the textures of silken smooth skin and the hard point of her nipple.

Mason bit her cheek as he held her, making a little growl of pleasure. Jasmine took a sharp breath, but she moved against him, running her hands down Mason's back to cup his backside.

Life was fragile. Mason had learned that lesson very young. He'd learned to savor moments such as these as he came upon them—the sound of a beautifully made instrument, the light that could paint the Texas skies a brilliant shade of gold, the taste of this woman rising to desire.

Mason flicked his thumb across her nipple, liking how it tightened still more, matching the hardening of his cock. He moved her backward to the bed, and Jasmine gave a little laugh as she reached the edge of the bed and began to fall backward.

He lowered her gently until she was lying on the mattress, and Mason came down over her. He pushed up her shirt, baring her breasts to him. Mason saw that, as he'd thought, one of the tattooed vines snaked down her breast and encircled her nipple, a tiny flower peeking out under the areola.

Mason traced the end of the vine with his tongue, pressing a gentle kiss to the flower. Jasmine hummed in pleasure, and lifted her foot to caress the back of his leg, her sandal stiff on his thigh.

A cell phone rang. The bleating buzz cut the air, and Jasmine jerked under him.

Mason, his lips hovering above the tattooed vine, growled, "Ignore it."

Jasmine already had her fingers in his pocket, tugging the phone free. "It might be important," she said breathlessly.

Mason growled again then grabbed the flip phone from her and looked at the readout. His brother, Broderick.

"What?" he yelled into it.

"You find him yet?" Broderick's strident tones came through, loud enough to fill the room. Jasmine wriggled out from under Mason, sat up, and tugged her top down.

"No," Mason snapped. "I only started looking yesterday."

"I know that, but Aleck's getting worse. We might have to put him down after all."

Mason didn't like the note in Broderick's voice. "Why?" he demanded. "What did he do this time?"

"He went after Aunt Cora." Broderick quieted, his anger plain. "He hurt her bad. All this is my fucking fault."

"No it isn't." Mason stood up, leaving Jasmine's softness with regret. "It's the fault of his Shifter leader who couldn't keep him from going feral." He paused. "How bad is she?"

Mason's heart thumped as he waited for Broderick's answer. Auntie Cora had taken care of him — of the whole family — after their father's death when their mother had gone into her decline. Aunt Cora had looked after Mason most of all, knowing that a cub would need as much love and reassurance as he could get. Aunt Cora had been his mother longer than his true mother had been.

Broderick sounded vastly unhappy. "It's bad. I don't know if she'll make it." His voice faltered, then he continued. "Andrea has done what she can. Aunt Cora was defending Joanne from Aleck ..."

He broke off, his sudden silence holding fury and worry.

"Then we'll definitely need the Shifter healer," Mason said grimly. "I'm coming back there. I might have a lead, and I'll need all the resources we can get to follow it up."

***

Mason drove into Austin more hurriedly than he'd rolled out of it. Jasmine clung to his back as he dove off the back highway to the streets that led to Shiftertown late the next afternoon. He'd wanted to take Jasmine straight to the safe house he had in mind, but she insisted she accompany him home first.

"I need to see everything," she said. "Where you live, who lives with you, the man you're trying to heal ..."

Mason wasn't certain why, but he didn't argue too much. He'd seen the face in the smoke, and Jasmine had witnessed the exact same thing—they'd compared notes and agreed. Whatever Goddess magic had helped her, she'd found *someone*.

When Mason pulled up the drive of the big house, he found three Shifters on the porch who didn't belong there—Liam Morrissey; his father, Dylan; and the giant of a man called Tiger.

"What the hell?" Mason asked as he helped Jasmine off the bike. "Where's Broderick?"

As he took what he wanted out of the saddlebag and went up the porch steps, he heard a woman crying inside, and Joanne's voice, trying to console her.

Mason didn't like these Felines on his territory. Didn't matter that Liam was his Shiftertown leader, Dylan out-alphaed every Shifter in Hill Country and South Texas, and that Tiger could take out both of the other two without blinking.

Tiger answered before Liam could. "They want to cage him."

The disgust and anger in his voice was unmistakable. Tiger had spent the first forty years of his life, including his cub-hood and Transition, in a cage. Liam might have brought Tiger with him today to reinforce his decision to pen up Aleck, but Mason could see that Tiger was not happy with that solution.

"His mate asked for it," Liam explained, keeping his voice quiet. "She realizes that Aleck is too far gone. She knows he might hurt her next, and their unborn cub, and she feels terrible about Cora."

Jasmine hurried up onto the porch and around Mason before he could stop her. "Can I see him?" she asked Dylan, who blocked the doorway. "If I can keep an image of him in my head it might help me reach the healer—he might understand how much we need him."

Dylan, not answering, regarded Jasmine with unmoving blue eyes. Jasmine looked right back at him without fear.

She didn't know she was supposed to be afraid, Mason realized. For all her talk of dating a Shifter, she likely hadn't been around one as high in dominance as Dylan.

Mason usually had trouble meeting Dylan's gaze—he mostly didn't bother to try—but at this moment, seeing the man on his territory, staring down his mate, wiped away all trepidation.

Mason was in front of Jasmine in a heartbeat, giving Dylan a fierce look. *Back off.*

Dylan's brows went up, and Liam looked interested.

Jasmine, oblivious, had turned to Tiger. She stared up at him, her mouth open, and Tiger looked down at her, his golden eyes softening.

"Wow," Jasmine said. "Your aura is incredible." She lifted her hand and ran it through the air at Tiger's side. "So beautiful."

Tiger only watched her. Mason, who never, ever would have pitted himself against Tiger — he wasn't insane — shoved himself between Tiger and Jasmine. Tiger switched his intense gaze to Mason, looking deep into him in the crazy way he had.

Tiger studied Mason, flicked his focus back to Jasmine, then gave a slow nod and turned away.

Jasmine swung eagerly to Mason, not noticing how possessive he'd become. "What kind of Shifter is *he*?" She pointed at Tiger. "I've never seen anything like him."

"A tiger," Mason grunted. "We call him Tiger. I want to see Aunt Cora. Is Aleck secured yet?" he asked Liam.

"They have him in the basement," Liam answered. "It's bad, Mason. I'm sorry."

Heart pounding, Mason made his way into the house.

The living room and the rest of the first floor was empty, but Mason knew by scent where everyone was. He headed upstairs, and Jasmine came right behind him. Mason knew *her* scent and her presence, which wrapped him as though she held his hand.

Nancy, Aleck's mate, waited for them at the top of the stairs. Her abdomen protruded in the shirt and loose pants she wore, and her hand rested protectively on her belly. Her eyes were red-rimmed from weeping and held profound sadness.

"Mason, I'm so sorry," she whispered.

Jasmine slid a supporting arm around Nancy's waist. "Now then, young lady, you do not need to be up and wandering around while you're so upset. You'll tire out your baby. Let's get you somewhere you can rest, and I'll give you stones to hold that will ease you. Mason and I are going to find the healer who will fix all this, I promise you. I'm Jasmine, by the way, but everyone calls me Jazz."

Everyone except Mason. She'd always be *Jasmine* to him, a name that described her beauty and resilience.

It was in that moment that he realized that when he'd seen Dylan staring her down, he'd referred to her in his mind as his mate.

He pushed aside that startling thought as he entered Aunt Cora's room. Andrea was there at Aunt Cora's bed, as was Broderick's mate, Joanne. Andrea sat on the edge of the bed, gently adjusting bandages over Aunt Cora's torso.

In the corner, standing like a sentinel, was Sean, the Guardian. His sword rose above his shoulder, a reminder that death hovered near. Sean was there in case Aunt Cora slipped away, so he could drive that big sword through her heart and send her body to dust, releasing her spirit to the Summerland.

Mason's chest tightened until it ached. Aunt Cora's eyes were closed, her breathing shallow, her skin showing around the bandages covered with slashes and bite marks. Joanne moved out of the way when she saw Mason, and Mason reached down and took Aunt Cora's hand.

"Hey, Auntie," he said. "It's me. The runt of the litter."

Aunt Cora didn't respond. Andrea looked up at Mason and gave him the faintest shake of her head. Aunt Cora was alive, but they were expecting her to die.

"What happened?" Mason asked, steel in his voice.

Joanne answered, sounding tired. "Aleck got out of his room—he broke the chains on his bed like they were nothing. He went for me—I don't know why. Aunt Cora was the closest to me. She shifted to wolf and leapt to my defense. Aleck just attacked her. Broderick and his brothers were already coming up the stairs when it happened, and they got Aleck under control, but the damage had been done."

Mason nodded. A Feline going for the kill was swift and deadly. A Lupine sometimes decided to give an opponent a fighting chance, out of respect or for the hell of it, but cats mostly chose not to. Felines gutted their prey as quickly as possible, which was why they had been the favorite species of the Fae. There were many, many different Feline hybrids and crosses—sometimes referred to as Fae cats—while wolves and bears had only a few types and bred closer to the wild species.

Mason tried to hate Aleck for what he'd done, but he knew that it wasn't Aleck's fault. It was the fucked-up shit inside every Shifter's brain, put there eons ago by the Fae, and passed along in the genetic code through the generations. Shifters had been made to be killers after all.

Aunt Cora had behaved true when she'd turned on the Feline to protect Broderick's mate and unborn cub. Protecting the cubs was the strongest instinct every Shifter had, the instinct that had enabled them to get free from the Fae once and for all.

Mason didn't care about that shit right now. He only cared that Aunt Cora, the woman who'd taken care of him, easing his fears and pain when he'd been an unruly cub, was lying close to death. He couldn't lose her too.

Warmth touched his side then his hand as Jasmine slid her fingers around his. She looked up at him in perfect understanding.

Mason lifted the striped bag from Inspirations he'd brought in, took out the brightly wrapped box with the scarf in it, and laid it on the nightstand.

"Give that to her when she wakes up," he said to Joanne. He deliberately said *when* and not *if*.

Mason turned his back on the bed and walked out the door. In the hall, Jasmine stopped him from rushing down the stairs by putting her arms around him.

Her strength and caring came to him through the embrace. Mason leaned to her, accepting the hug and holding her tight in response, brushing a kiss to her soft hair. He could see her chocolate-brown roots up close, and nuzzled them.

"I promise you, Mason, I'll find this guy," Jasmine was saying as she held on. "I won't stop until I do. I swear this to you. Don't you worry, now."

***

Jazz hoped she hadn't been too optimistic about what help she could be to Mason. They didn't speak as they left the house and mounted the motorcycle again so Mason could take her to the safe house.

Broderick hadn't let them into the basement to see Aleck. Too dangerous, Broderick had said, since they didn't have him secure enough yet. It didn't matter, Jazz realized. Aleck's aura permeated the house, the darkness of it swallowing up any brightness that had been in it.

Broderick looked much like Mason, Jazz noted. He was an older version of his youngest brother, more world-weary, but his aura also bore the contentment of a man who'd found his life-mate and would soon have a child. Worry for them overlaid his aura as well.

Jazz hung on to Mason as he rode through and out of downtown Austin, the tall buildings up and down the river flashing past. On the west side of town, he left the main streets and moved through a neighborhood of old bungalows from early in the last century. The houses were buried among huge trees, and screened from the hurrying city by more trees and high hedges.

The house Mason took Jazz to was nearly hidden from the street and reached by steps set into the side of a hill.

Someone had been sprucing up the place. The outside had been freshly painted, a porch swing hung near the front door, and brightly flowering plants dangled from hooks and rested in flower boxes.

The inside didn't have much furniture, Jazz saw after Mason checked out the house and let her in, but a table and chairs rested near a window, the westering sun giving the room plenty of light.

"Who lives here?" Jazz asked as she looked around in delight. The feel of the bungalow was homey but secluded.

"No one," Mason said as he came back into the living room. "Everyone. It's a house where Shifters can come if they need to be alone. That knowledge isn't public."

Jazz warmed that he'd share a secret with her and held up her hand. "I promise by the Goddess I'll never tell another living soul about it."

"Don't promise," Mason said quickly. He picked up her bag and his duffel that he'd left on the porch and deposited them near the table. "What if you find a Shifter in trouble who needs somewhere to go?"

Jazz considered. "All right—I promise never to tell unless I stumble across a Shifter who is in dire need of a place to stay. Okay?"

Mason turned in a circle as though checking the room again, then he collapsed into one of the chairs.

"Sure. Fine."

Jazz's heart hurt for him. Mason had looked gray-faced and crushed when he'd stood next to his aunt's bed and realized she might not survive. Jazz knew that look and the feeling—she'd had it when she'd held her grandmother's hand as she'd slipped away.

"I really do have some ideas for how to find the healer," Jazz said, trying to sound reassuring. "Though I could use a burger or something before I get to them."

Mason shook himself. "Yeah, there's food." He moved off toward the kitchen, but absently, his energy gone. His aura reflected it, a somber yellow instead of hot fire.

Jazz opened her bag and took out her things, laying them out as she had in the motel room. She'd carefully wrapped the bowl that held the charred remains of the sage stick, and now she set it in the very center of her velvet cloth. There had been a connection between her and Mason and the man in the smoke, she knew it.

But first—sustenance. Her grandmother had taught her that being undernourished and tired drained psychic energy and kept Jazz from being her very best. Jazz had the feeling she'd have to be at peak performance to help Mason and the poor woman lying in the bed across town.

They ate the delicious cheeseburgers Mason prepared for them on the indoor grill—the house was well stocked. What lucky Shifter woman would win this man who kissed like fire, had the body of a god, and was a fantastic cook as well? Jazz thought wistfully that the woman would be fortunate indeed.

After they finished, Mason took the leavings of dinner back to the kitchen, and Jazz turned to her divining tools. The sun had set, the moon rising—all the better. The moon was the symbol of the Goddess, and Jazz needed all the help she could get. In the motel in northeast Texas, she'd needed all the elements—earth, air, fire, water—plus the blessings of the Goddess to discover even the small amount of information she had.

Jazz privately thought she wouldn't have managed a connection to the healer at all if Mason hadn't been there. She'd been doing divination since she was very young, learning all her grandmother had to teach her until she was well adept, but she'd never had a manifestation that sharp and clear before. Mason's strength and power, even when he'd dozed on the other side of the room, had helped her tap an ability she hadn't realized she had.

When Mason returned from the kitchen, Jazz asked him to sit across from her and place his hands on the table, while she laid out the stones in front of him.

She liked having Mason close, helping her work, though he might not believe in what she did. However, he'd lost his former cynicism and now silently touched stones as she instructed or waved his hand above the sage smoke, never questioning why.

His presence calmed her. Jazz took in his strong body, his blunt-fingered hands that had brushed over her guitar with such care and now rested lightly on the stones. Those same hands had gently cupped her breasts, bringing her to life. He studied the stones on the cloth, his lashes flicking as he looked down at them.

Jazz pulled her thoughts back to the cards she'd spread on the table in front of the stones. It was difficult to concentrate—she was so tired and the man in front of her was hard to ignore.

She tried to scold herself that he was *Shifter*, and she was never going there again.

But Mason was hot, desirable, as lonely as she was, and three feet away from her.

Jazz firmed her jaw and went back to her whispered prayers to the Goddess as she laid down the next cards.

Every single one was a blockage, or a positive card reversed. The Tower again, and the Devil. The stones' auras remained dark, the candles guttered and died, and the pathetic wisp of smoke that came from her bowl of sage drifted apart and showed her nothing.

Finally Jazz cried out in frustration and swept her hand across the table, scattering crystals, salt, incense sticks, and cards to the floor.

"Damn it!" she cried. "I don't know what I'm doing wrong. This should *work*!"

Jazz beat on the table, which she knew wouldn't help, but despair flanked her and took away all hope. She'd done everything the same as she had in the motel room, but this time there was no spark, no feeling of knowledge, no connection. Jazz stilled her hands and rested her forehead on them, letting out a groan.

Mason's arms closed around her from behind, his warmth easing her. His lips on her hair quieted her anger but began to awaken something else.

No. Jazz wouldn't let herself fall for a Shifter. Not again. It was just too painful.

Good intentions went to the wind as Mason lifted her from the seat, gathering her back against him. His mouth on her neck made her skin prickle with excited heat, and she felt his hardness against the small of her back.

Mason turned her in his arms, his mouth coming down on hers, and Jazz didn't resist very much. Pointless, really.

Chapter Nine

Mason carried Jasmine upstairs, his heart beating thickly.

Though he'd never spent the night here, he knew exactly where the bedrooms were and which one had the largest bed. He'd helped Seamus work on the place, painting and drywalling, stocking the kitchen, and he'd learned every part of the house.

Mason took Jasmine into the small room under the eaves, the slanting beamed ceiling giving it an old-fashioned look.

The feel of the bungalow had changed since the first time he'd entered it. Before, it had held tension, worry, as Shifters Seamus needed to hide had stayed here for a time. Now it was far more peaceful, a haven for Shifters to come to get away and meditate or whatever. Sex took place here—Mason's brothers liked to use the house to enjoy themselves in private. Broderick sometimes brought Joanne out here—not that Mason blamed him. It was quiet, soothing, the walls embracing.

Mason reflected he was getting to be able to read houses as well as Jasmine read cards. At least this one didn't try to eat people. Well, not so far.

Jasmine smiled at Mason as though she knew his thoughts. Moonlight shone through the uncurtained window, the round disk almost full. The silver light touched Jasmine's face and dark blue eyes, enhancing her beauty.

Mason laid Jasmine on the bed. She rose on her elbows, watching him.

"Mason, I—"

Mason leaned down and touched his finger to her lips. "Nothing to say."

"But—"

He pressed a little harder. If Jasmine started questioning, or explaining, Mason might believe he had no business being with her and talk himself out of it.

"We're here," he said softly. Mason removed his finger and kissed lightly where he'd touched. "Now. That's all that matters."

"I like that." Jasmine's breath brushed his lips.

Mason resisted kissing her again and stepped back to slide off his shirt. Jasmine leaned back again, studying him with flattering interest.

"This is nice," she said. "I always wanted a gorgeous guy doing a striptease for me."

Mason flushed, face hot. "I don't dance." He unbuckled, unbuttoned, and unzipped his jeans as fast as possible and shoved them down his legs, not bothering with elegance.

Jasmine's gaze moved to his underwear and the hardness he could no longer hide. Her eyes widened when he simply slid off the underwear, his heavy cock tumbling out.

Mason saw no need to be embarrassed about his body and his wanting. How could he not want Jasmine? Her posture thrust her breasts forward a little, her nipples pressing the thin shirt.

Her long legs awaited his touch. Mason stepped to the bed and slid his hands up them, finding the heat and softness of her inner thighs. Jasmine made a noise of contentment, a sound that wrapped Mason's wanting and heightened it.

One thing did embarrass him, though, and he found himself needing to tell her.

"I haven't been with many women," Mason said in a rush. He lifted his hands from her and stood up. "I'm not long past my Transition. But Shifters are kind of programmed to ... it's instinctive ..." *To screw as often as possible until we have cubs. It's all we want.*

No, that couldn't be true. Mason wanted *Jasmine*, no matter whether they mated and had cubs. He wanted her with growing frenzy, didn't matter how inexperienced he was.

Jasmine looked at him in wonder. She sat up, touching his clenched fist. "Wait, are you saying you're a virgin? Seriously?"

"Almost," Mason answered, his frenzy growing until he wasn't interested in the discussion anymore. He'd had an encounter with a female Lupine for a few weeks right after his Transition—she'd been from another Shiftertown—but he'd been young and uncertain, and the whole thing had ended quickly.

He'd never seen her again, and there's been no question of a mate bond. Groupies at Shifter bars wanted Mason and told him so, but he couldn't dredge up any enthusiasm for them.

Jasmine lost her smile and tugged Mason a little closer. "I'm glad, actually. I don't want to be one in a long chain. Another notch on a bedpost."

"Shifters who do that are stupid," Mason said without hesitation. "Every act of lovemaking should be special. Shifters never know when we'll form the mate bond. I'd rather form it with a woman I took time to be with instead of having blown her off in a one-night stand. I'd be hearing about *that* for the rest of my life."

"You know, I really do like you." Jasmine pulled him closer, running her hands up his torso as she stood and slid her arms around his waist, kissing him again.

Mason loosened her shirt as he leaned into her, his hands pulling it off. His kisses turned urgent, and he gathered her against him, loving the feel of her breasts against his chest. He moved one hand to her waistband and then jumped as her cool fingers closed around his cock.

The sound in his throat was primal. Mason tugged open Jasmine's shorts and sank his fingers into her heat.

Jasmine's answering groan slid into Mason's head and sent his body into crazed need. He pushed her shorts and underwear all the way down and turned with her in his arms. Jasmine still had hold of his cock, the little smile on her lips when he kissed her again telling him she liked what was in her hands.

Mason slid his fingers once more to the space between her legs, making her lips part, dissolving the smile. Jasmine got an *oh, yeah?* look on her face, and skimmed her hand up his cock from base to tip.

Mason jerked, and tried to back away. But he'd have to let go of her to do so, and Jasmine wouldn't release him. "You're killing me," he said savagely. His mating frenzy pounded through him, sending his heartbeat searingly high.

"What do you think you're doing to *me*?" Jasmine demanded.

She abruptly turned and sat on the bed, but she didn't release Mason. She tugged at him, and Mason had no choice but to go to her.

He pushed her back into the mattress, arranging her so she lay full length on the bed. Jasmine lost hold of him but she latched on to his cock again as he lay down on her.

"Witch," he said with a growl.

"Psychic," Jasmine countered.

Mason could have made some kind of a joke about predicting what would happen next, but he had no more interest in teasing. He touched Jasmine's face as she lay under him, enjoying the satin feel of her skin.

"You're beautiful," Mason said softly. "The minute I saw you, I ... changed."

Mason wasn't certain what he meant, but Jasmine's eyes warmed. Mason had seen her beauty, the openness of her. He ran his fingertips from her arm to her breast, tracing the flowers and vines, then he leaned down, as he had in the motel room, and traced them again with his tongue.

Jasmine relaxed beneath him, letting out an *mmm* of contentment.

The taste of her, a mixture of salty and sweet, built the need to touch, lick, kiss this woman. Mason moved his mouth between her breasts, kissing there, then drawing his tongue all the way up to her throat.

Jasmine's chest rose with her breath, her hands coming up to stroke Mason's back. His heart pounded, his cock aching as it brushed between her thighs, feeling the same damp heat his fingers had found.

Jasmine smiled up at him, moonlight catching in her blue eyes, her short hair casting black streaks over her cheeks. Mason nuzzled locks of hair aside, kissing her face, her chin, back to her throat.

A longing to be inside her gripped him and didn't let go. No need in his life had been this intense, not even the natural frenzy that took hold of him just after his Transition. Then he'd wanted *something* but didn't really know how to find it. Now he knew — it was Jasmine.

She touched his face, drew her hand down his side, snaked it around to his cock again. Mason groaned as her fingers danced on him, thumb sliding over his tip.

Damn it. Mason yanked himself away from her, rolling off the bed and standing upright, while Jasmine looked at him in surprise.

"I can't go slow if you touch me like that," Mason said, his voice hoarse. "I'll just take you."

"I like slow." Jasmine touched her finger to her lips. Whether she did that on purpose to bait him, or unconsciously, it was erotic as hell. "Fast can be good too."

She reached for his hand, but Mason backed away. If he came to her now, he'd simply thrust inside, spend himself, and collapse. He didn't want to be clumsy, rushed. He wanted to savor.

His body was having other ideas. Mason clenched his fists, his temperature soaring, skin damp. He made himself walk to the nightstand, where he knew his brothers kept a stash of condoms, opened the drawer, and withdraw one. They were large enough for Shifters—his horny brother Derek would ensure that.

Jasmine said nothing about the condom. She lifted on her elbows again, watching as Mason tore the packet open and rolled it on. The touch of cold latex was annoying but didn't dampen the heat that roiled through him.

"I could help you with that, you know," Jasmine said softly. "More fun."

Mason had no idea women even wanted to touch the things. Next time. He was already determined there would be a next time.

Mason came down to her. He wanted to be bare against her, nothing between them, but he'd wait until they were officially mated. Then there would be no barrier, and they'd let frenzy take them all night and all day.

Jasmine's face changed from smiles and teasing to need that matched his own. Mason nudged her knees open, lowering himself all the way on top of her. His experience was very slight, but he had older brothers who had never held back their graphic descriptions.

Mason knew exactly how to position himself, bracing his fists against the mattress, and slide inside her.

Jasmine let out a faint cry, her eyes half closing, her hips rocking up as though she couldn't help herself. Mason pressed all the way in ...

And everything in the world suddenly became sharp and clear. Fog rolled away from his mind, as though all that he'd seen before had been only half formed.

Wild sensation began where they joined in one hot point, then traveled through his body, lightning streaks of fiery joy. Mason looked down at Jasmine, seeing all of her for the first time—her beauty both in her body and deep inside her.

Goddess, if he'd known loving a woman would be like *this*, he wouldn't have waited.

But no, this was Jasmine. Worth the wait.

Mason drew in a long breath, exhaling onto her skin, touching her with his scent. *Mine.*

He'd thought the feeling he drowned in was the best life could offer. That is, until he drew back and thrust again.

Astonishing awareness washed over him, streaking down every nerve, building fire all the way to his fingertips.

He thought *that* feeling the best in the world just before Jasmine squeezed down on him. Mason let out a cross between a shout and a groan. *Goddess, Goddess, thank you.*

His thoughts scattered, and sensation took over. So did frenzy. Mason lost coherence, only knowing the softness of Jasmine, the scent of her, her heat that filled him even as he filled her.

He thrust again and again, knowing sounds came out of his mouth, blending with the little noises of pleasure that came out of Jasmine's. She held him tightly, fingers pressing, urging him on, her frenzy as great as his. Her hair tangled on the pillow, her blue eyes captured him, and moonlight brushed them both.

Mason's world went through upheaval again as he spiraled to the point of his coming. Jasmine moved beneath him, her breasts against his chest, the points of her nipples tight. She was coming under him, the rock of her hips, her sudden cries of joy making her even hotter where he thrust into her.

Her pressure around him, the sweet sounds she made, her warmth and fragrance, shoved Mason over the top. He came and came, pounding the mattress with his fist, his body shuddering and moving.

Jasmine was right there with him, their bodies sealed together, she coming off the bed to meld with him for their final thrusts.

Mason crashed down on her, his blood searing, the astonishing joy that flooded him erasing everything he'd previously understood and filling him with new knowledge.

Then he was just Mason, kissing and laughing with the beautiful Jasmine, touching her in the moonlight, the Goddess silently blessing them.

***

When Jazz opened her eyes some time later, her body limp and more relaxed than it had been in her life, she found Mason propped on his side next to her, staring down at her. His gray eyes were soft, the edge of him gone.

"Hey," he said.

"I fell asleep," Jazz mumbled, still halfway there.

"Yeah, you did." Mason kissed her forehead with gentle lips. At some point, he'd rid himself of the condom, and his warm cock, as hard as ever, bumped her thigh.

"Sorry."

"No." Mason smoothed her hair from her face. "You're beautiful when you sleep."

Jazz put a self-conscious hand to her cheek. "No drooling?"

The bed shook with Mason's laughter. "Not this time."

He was breathtaking when he smiled. She'd seen him do it so rarely, but it lit his eyes, made him more devastatingly handsome than ever.

"You sure don't have a lot of experience?" Jazz asked him. "Seemed like you knew what you were doing."

Mason shrugged, which moved him in a fine way. "My brothers talk about it constantly. Even when I was a cub and had no clue what it meant, they went on and on about it."

"I guess it rubbed off." Jazz stroked her fingers over his arm. "I'm glad. You kind of blew me away, you know."

Mason looked slightly surprised, but Jazz hadn't exaggerated. It had *never* felt like that before.

"We should probably go downstairs and start searching again," she said without enthusiasm. People were counting on her and her abilities. But lying here, being touched by Mason and his wonderful aura, was the best thing that had ever happened to her.

"Not yet." Mason's strong hand pushed her down. "I need this. Life. You."

Jazz understood, and shared the feeling. The fear, rage, grief, worry that had hovered over Mason's house had helped drive them into each other's arms, both of them needing solace, comfort, hope.

She wished she could tell him not to bother with the condom again, but neither of them knew what the future would bring. Jazz said nothing as he opened the nightstand drawer. This time, though, she eased it onto him herself, and it did prove to be much more fun.

Jazz knew that by the way Mason had her down on the bed in two seconds, thrusting inside her as she let the foil wrapper flutter to the floor.

Then nothing mattered but Mason's weight on her, the fullness of him inside her, and the wild light in his wolf-gray eyes.

***

Mason woke to a faint glow. He assumed it dawn until he looked at the window and found it still dark. His internal clock told him it was only about four in the morning, but something was shining and shining hard.

Jasmine slept on next to him, undisturbed. Mason looked down at her a moment, his entire body rejoicing in the nearness of her. The sensation of her around him, of being inside her, remained strong, the fierce longing being with her had ignited undimmed.

He would have woken her with kisses, slid inside her, and sought that tearing joy of being with her again except for whatever light was pulsating downstairs.

Mason carefully slid from the bed, not wanting to alarm Jasmine. Without bothering to dress — clothes would get in the way if he had to shift — he moved to the tiny hall, saw that the glow was coming from below, and moved stealthily down the staircase.

He didn't scent an intruder, but that didn't mean no one was there. There were various ways to fool a Shifter's sense of smell, though those at least alerted a Shifter that there was something wrong. The house smelled empty except for himself and Jasmine. Felt empty.

Mason made it to the first floor and slipped into deeper shadow, avoiding the faint glimmer from the streetlight.

The vibrating glow was coming from the floor of the living room. Jasmine had flung most of her stones to the carpet in her anguish, her velvet cloth landing on top of them. Now the cloth itself seemed to be radiating light.

Mason moved on wary feet across the carpet then ever so cautiously, leaned down and lifted the velvet.

Every stone underneath it was awash with light. The heart of each — amethyst, obsidian, red jasper, amber, rose quartz, turquoise — blazed fire, bathing Mason's skin in blue, pink, yellow, red, purple. The amber in particular was shining hard, brushing Mason's outstretched hand with a golden hue.

One of the stones moved, or so Mason thought. He backed off, not trusting rocks that suddenly shone with intrinsic light.

No, they *were* moving. Little by little, as though tremors rocked them, the stones wriggled, sliding forward. But only the stones. The rest of the house was utterly still.

Mason growled. The wolf in him bristled as he watched the stones roll and vibrate toward the map that had also fallen to the floor.

He needed to wake Jasmine. Mason started to turn, but found his feet rooted to the carpet. He struggled, but damned if he could move. The light from the amber grew brighter and brighter, engulfing him, until Mason could no longer see anything else.

Only one thing to do. Mason surrendered to the wolf inside him and let himself change.

Chapter Ten

Jazz woke to the snarling that filled the house. She reached for Mason next to her to find him gone, the warm indentation in the mattress the only evidence he'd been there. Been there to touch her, bring her to life, awaken a passion that had been dormant in her for so long. He'd punched past her fears, her insecurities, and made love to her with a fire she'd never forget.

The growls escalated and Jazz came all the way awake. She snatched up her underwear and Mason's T-shirt and jerked them on before she scurried from the little bedroom and down the stairs.

The staircase in this house emptied right into the living room. A large wolf stood in the middle of it, his gray and white fur bathed in a yellow glow. Crystals surrounded the wolf, forming a circle with him furious in its center.

Jazz watched, openmouthed, as the remainder of her stones gathered in a corner of the map, jostling each other madly as though trying to rest on the same point.

Mason kept growling. The rumbling of it filled the room and shook her bones.

Jazz made herself break out of her standstill and run to the map. She didn't dare snap on a lamp or even light a candle. Magic was fragile, and any disturbance could negate the process.

She didn't need light anyway. Her stones were beaming so intensely that they threw sharp, colorful shadows over the room. The stones had gathered on the map of Alaska, trembling and struggling to remain on a dot they covered in their enthusiasm.

Mason seemed unable to move. Jazz watched the wolf's body jerk as he tried to get free, snarled when he couldn't. The amber stone sat right in front of Mason, its light the brightest. It made his gray fur golden and glittered in his enraged eyes.

Jazz knew that if she snatched up the stone, whatever magic was flowing between it and Mason would cease. The stone's aura had connected with something in Mason's, the innate magic Jazz had sensed inside him the moment they'd met. Mason was Shifter, yes, but there was more to him than that.

The wolf glared at Jazz, clearly telling her to shut off the stone and let him loose, but Jazz made a wide berth around him and dropped to her hands and knees next to the map. She didn't touch it, knowing that any interference could switch off the magic in an instant.

The stones hid the point they gathered over, an area north and west of Anchorage. Not terribly specific, but it was a start.

Jazz turned excitedly to Mason. "Alaska. I *knew* it."

Mason continued to growl, a wolf enraged. He wanted to attack something, probably the amber that kept him hostage, but he could do nothing.

"Hang on," Jazz said. "I want to try something. You're a powerful magic beacon, and I don't want to switch you off yet."

She scrambled to the table and grabbed her notebook and pencil, one of the few things she hadn't thrown to the floor. Jazz got to her knees again and quickly sketched the map and the position of the stones.

She passed her hands through the air over the quivering stones, formed an image of the Goddess in her head, and said, "Reveal."

The amber light around Mason became blindingly white. Jazz shielded her eyes while the stones next to her also flared, sending multicolored light over Jazz, Mason's black T-shirt, the notebook, and the growling wolf. Jazz jammed her hand to the paper, willing the pencil point to write, draw, make a dot, *something,* to show her where they needed to go.

The stones rocked and wriggled, their light growing brighter and brighter, heating the air. The map burst into flames, the sudden puff of fire throwing Jazz backward. The carpet caught and began to burn with enthusiasm.

Jazz yelped, grabbed the velvet cloth, and tried to smother the flames. The cloth itself caught fire, and she scrambled back from it.

Mason was snarling and snapping, his ears back, fangs bared. Jazz hurried to him and kicked the amber stone away from him.

The glow didn't die. The fire on the floor started to catch in earnest.

Jazz dove for the piece of amber, drew it back, and threw it into the heart of the flame. She had no idea what made her do that, but every instinct told her it was right.

Each color of light burst upward, filling the room with radiant beauty and heat, then suddenly all light died. One instant, a rainbow infused the house, the next, it was utterly dark, the only light the yellow glare of the still-burning carpet. Mason, freed, turned around and dashed out of the room.

Phone. Jazz needed a phone, needed to call the fire department.

There was no land line that she could see by the light of the flames in the living room. Her cell phone was upstairs, but a streak of flame began to zip between her and the staircase. She'd have to run to the nearest neighbor and hope they didn't hate Shifters.

Mason charged back into the room at that moment, an unclothed human man with a fire extinguisher in his hands. He aimed it at the burning carpet, smothering the flames in white foam.

A few seconds later, Jazz was coughing at the smell of charred rug, the room now lighted only by the yellowish streetlight at the bottom of the front yard.

Mason switched off the extinguisher and let it hang from his big hand. He breathed hard, his bare skin gleaming with perspiration.

Jazz put her hands on her hips, looked him up and down, and let out a shaky laugh. "Well, that's something I don't see every day."

"What?" Mason scowled at her. "Stones catching your house on fire? Or a Shifter who knows how to use a fire extinguisher?" Mason gazed down at the damp and stinking patch of smoldered carpet. "Aw, Seamus is going to kill me."

Jazz had meant a hot-bodied, naked man running to her rescue, but she said instead, "You — lit up with amazing magic." Her excitement made her laugh. "And then be only worried about the stupid carpet. You're the most incredible man I've ever met."

Mason looked at her, his gray eyes steady under his formidable frown. "Bet you say that to all Shifters who glow."

"Only you. You really are astonishing, Mason." Jazz pressed her hands together. "I really, really didn't want you near me at first, but I'm so glad I met you." She squeezed her palms, making her fingers bite into her hands to keep her grounded in reality. "Even when you find your true Shifter mate and disappear from my life, I'll still be happy I connected with you. You've made me realize that not all Shifters are so bad." Her heart ached to think of the day she'd say good-bye to Mason, but she wasn't such a fool to believe that sleeping with him meant they were bound together forever. That wasn't how it worked for Shifters.

Mason's sudden growl made her jump. He'd made that noise when he was wolf. Hearing it coming from his human mouth was scary.

"*Don't* tell me where I'm going to form the mate bond," Mason said, his voice fierce. "Or that I'll disappear anytime soon." He moved to her, dumping the extinguisher as he went. "I'm not letting *you* out of my sight."

Jazz sucked in a breath as he wrapped his arms around her and lifted her from her feet. Mason's growls softened as he drew Jazz against him and kissed the corner of her mouth.

His eyes held the fire of the amber. Jazz knew good and well that the magic that had sent the stones to tell her where the healer was had been his, not hers.

That thought slid to the back of her mind as Mason's kiss opened her, his hands gripping through the shirt. His skin was smooth and hot, his cock hard with renewed arousal.

They barely made it to the bedroom this time. Mason had Jazz down on the mattress before she knew it, and before long was buried deep inside her.

Jazz lifted herself to him and gave of herself, pushing aside any worries of the future. She wanted the here and now, and she let herself drown in it.

***

"Alaska," Liam Morrissey said. "Are you certain, lad?"

Mason nodded, holding in his impatience. "If Jasmine says Alaska, then it's Alaska."

Jasmine, sitting next to him at the closed bar for the Shifter meeting the next morning, said, "Oh, yes. The Goddess definitely pointed that way. I can only narrow it down to about a hundred mile radius, but it's a place to start."

Liam and the other Shifters in the bar didn't believe it, Mason saw. Or they wanted to but feared false hope. Jasmine, on the other hand, trusted what the Goddess had revealed with all her heart.

"I saw the stones and the map," Mason said in a hard voice. "There's no doubt."

"Aye, and there's a hole burned in the rug," Seamus said, both humor and annoyance in his tone. "Bree's not going to be happy about that, I have to warn you."

"I'll make it up to her," Jasmine said. "Is she doing all right?"

"She's devastated she couldn't come today," Seamus answered. "She says when she feels better you two will make a night of it. Which makes me worry, I have to say."

Jasmine grinned at him. "I'm thrilled with *why* Bree is indisposed today. I warned her about getting too involved with Shifters, but I take it back. I can tell you're good to her. Your aura is powerful, and a little ... different."

"That's why Bree likes me." Seamus fixed Jasmine with unblinking tawny eyes. "I'm different."

"Well, she's lucky," Jasmine said. "I'll tell her."

Seamus gave her his enigmatic smile, and Mason tried to tamp down his irritation. Jasmine was an open and engaging woman, and the Shifters here were already reacting to that. They liked her, and not just because Bree and Seamus vouched for her.

Mason wanted to gather her against him and tell all the others to back off. He'd found her, he'd breathed her scent and held her next to him, making love to her several more times this morning. He hadn't been able to stop, couldn't fill himself with enough of her to let his frenzy slack off. As Mason looked at Jasmine now, taking in her ragged black hair, delicate tattoos, and her warm smile, he knew he'd never have enough of her.

His need for her made him more aware of the Shifters around him. Some of Liam's trackers weren't yet mated, and this beautiful woman claiming they had terrific auras would set off their frenzy for certain.

The only one who seemed to notice Mason's growing unease and anger was Tiger. The big man turned his head and looked over at Mason as though sensing his thoughts.

"Tiger should go find this guy," Mason blurted into the discussion, making Liam, Dylan, and the other Shifters stop and stare at him. "Tiger's like a super-tracker, right? Made for search and rescue. If anyone can find a lone Shifter hiding in the Alaskan wilderness, it's Tiger."

"No," Tiger said without hesitation. He looked straight at Mason, pinning him with his unwavering golden gaze. "It has to be you."

Mason scowled, but at the same time he felt a strange flutter in his heart and knew that Tiger was right. Why Mason thought that or what the hell Tiger even meant, he didn't know, but the wolf in him agreed.

Damn it, Mason hated when his wolf thoughts and his human ones didn't mesh. Made him feel like the rope in someone else's game of tug-of-war.

"I need Tiger here," Dylan was saying in a calm voice. Dylan had been very quiet when Mason had presented what he and Jasmine had discovered, only watching Jasmine as she excitedly backed up Mason's story. "I can't spare him."

Tiger made no response, didn't look at Dylan, didn't argue one way or the other. Mason knew, however, that if Tiger had wanted to go to Alaska, nothing Dylan said would have prevented him. Tiger was staying here because *he* chose.

"Mason and I already know what this healer looks like," Jasmine was saying to Dylan, not flinching at all when he flicked his blue gaze to her. "There can't be that many Shifters in the area if there's no Shiftertown. Mason pointed out that the healer wasn't wearing a Collar, so he could be living in a human town, but I'll be able to track down his aura. Shifter auras are pretty obvious."

She glanced around the room, wrinkling her nose above her smile, as though implying that the auras in this room were thick. And they were—at least the scent was. A dozen nervous Shifters in an enclosed space could be ... intense.

Liam unfolded his arms. "Lad, if you want to go up to Alaska and try to find this man, I won't stop you. It's a long shot, but we've nothing to lose. I'll set up the transport for you and Jasmine, if she wants to accompany you."

Jasmine raised her brows. "Of course I want to go. Why wouldn't I?"

"Because," Mason said before Liam could answer, "it's a long and arduous trip, and they think it's a wild goose chase. You can stay here and hang out with Bree, and I'll go up and look around. Less dangerous for you if I get caught."

Jasmine gave Mason an incredulous look. "Don't be stupid. Of course, I'm going with you. You can't find the healer without me, and I can't find him without you. We need each other. He's there, Mason. It doesn't matter what anyone else believes."

Confidence radiated from her, the knowledge that the psychic world hadn't let her down. Her surety touched Mason, making him believe as well, and making him want to kiss the lips that curved in self-assuredness.

Liam gave Mason a nod. Mason could tell Liam wasn't certain Jasmine was right, but at least he was willing to provide the resources to help them search.

Or, maybe Liam was simply keeping Mason and Jasmine busy while he decided what he truly wanted to do. Liam didn't always broadcast his decisions at large.

"Two for Alaska, then," Liam said. "I suggest you pack warm."

The other Shifters relaxed and began to talk—or they simply left. Liam had decided, and the meeting was done.

Jasmine slipped from her chair and approached Tiger. Tiger waited for her, not moving as she stopped right in front of him.

"Even if you can't come with us, can you give us some direction?" Jasmine asked him. "I'm fairly confident I can find him now, but I'll take any help I can get."

Tiger gazed down at her for a long time. His mottled orange and black hair caught the fluorescent lights, but his large body stilled as he watched Jasmine.

Tiger shook his head ever so slightly. "It has to be you and Mason," he said. "Or it doesn't count."

Chapter Eleven

Mason scowled at Tiger. "Count for what, big guy? Or does that just mean you don't know?"

Tiger didn't move, paying no attention to Mason's surliness. "Shifter healers stay hidden because they feel too much pain. The need for them must be great, and only those with great need can find them."

Mason's impatience rose. "How do you know that? Or is it more of the cryptic shit programmed into your head?"

Tiger turned to Mason, unblinking. "It's in the Guardian database. Sean told me." He looked back at Jasmine. "And if I went with you, I would be—what does Carly call it? A fifth wheel."

Jasmine flushed. "No, you wouldn't ..."

Tiger sent her a wise look. "You and Mason want to be alone, and I don't want to leave Carly. She is carrying my cub." A note of extreme pride entered his voice. "You will succeed, and return with the healer."

"Well, I'm glad *someone* has confidence in us." Jasmine reached out and patted Tiger's arm. "Thank you. And congratulations on the cub. Kids are great."

Mason came alert as Jasmine's fingers brushed Tiger's large forearm. Tiger wasn't as comfortable with touching and hugging as other Shifters were, except with Carly, his mate, and very few others he trusted.

But Tiger simply looked at Jasmine, his eyes revealing that he was pleased with her and with himself. Without another word, Tiger turned and walked away, ducking out the door into the morning sunshine.

"Whew," Jasmine said, watching him go. "I like him. Nice of him to believe we can do this."

Mason shook his head. "He wasn't being polite. I don't think Tiger understands how to be. He can calculate odds like no one you'll ever meet. He's got numbers or something running in his head like a computer program." Mason waved his finger over his own temple. "He's never wrong."

"Good," Jasmine said brightly. She slid next to Mason and rose on tiptoe to kiss his cheek. "Then let's go find your healer."

***

In the few hours they had before the plane would arrive to carry them to Alaska, Mason took Jazz to the warehouse district of Austin and led her into a workshop in the corner of one of the large buildings.

Jazz immediately knew the place was his, even before they entered. She understood now where the creative streak in his aura had come from—the workshop held the matching vibrations. The feel of the cool room, the scent of wood and machinery, all matched Mason and his energy.

Jazz looked around at the standing band saws, scroll saws, drill press, lathe, and other machines she couldn't identify, as well as the hand tools scattered on the benches. Filing, sanding, and shaping tools were the most abundant. The faint odor of polish lingered in the air.

"You love it here," Jazz said in new understanding.

"I guess," Mason answered. His face was flushed, and for the first time since Jazz had met him, he looked shy.

"You really do. I can tell."

Mason answered her by sliding his arm around her and pulling her to him for a hot kiss. His kisses had changed, from newness and introduction to passion and a taste of afterglow.

Not that Jazz minded. She rose into the kiss, accepting and wanting, letting his lips play on hers.

When they finally parted, Mason had heat in his eyes and the territorial look she'd seen when they'd been among other Shifters. Though Dale, her Shifter ex, had been protective of her, he'd never studied Jazz with that kind of tense possessiveness.

Mason let her go, turning to unpack the Martin.

Jazz wandered the shop, looking over the couple of guitars in the making and a half-completed box of inlaid wood. The box was fairly large, about eight inches by four on the sides, four inches deep. "What will be in here?" she asked, touching it.

"Music box," Mason said. He carefully laid out the pieces of broken guitar on a workbench.

The box's lid had been inlaid in a chevron pattern of ebony and a lighter wood, bordered by a strip of mother-of-pearl. "It's beautiful. What will it play?"

"Haven't decided yet." Mason didn't look over at her. "Something classical like Mozart or Chopin."

"I like Bach," Jazz said peering at the box's polished but empty insides.

"Johann Sebastian or Johann Christian?"

Jazz came to him, giving him a blank look. "There's more than one?"

Mason kept his gaze on the guitar, but Jazz saw a flash of grin. "Christian was Sebastian's son. One of the many. Also known as the London Bach. He was a big influence on Mozart." Mason looked up again, the grin wry. "Yeah, the dumb-ass Shifter knows about eighteenth-century composers."

"Makes sense if you have to put their music in your boxes." Jazz glanced at a finished guitar hanging above the bench. It was made of a dark, striped wood she couldn't identify. "I never knew Shifters could be so artistic," she confessed.

"That's because you only met Shifters looking to pick up human women in bars," Mason said. "Shifters are horny. The ones in bars and roadhouses are looking for a quick screw, not a mating for life."

Jazz stilled, her heart constricting. "Which one do *you* want?"

Mason met her gaze, losing all teasing, all embarrassment. "We're not talking about me."

Not an answer. Jazz cleared her throat. "I really like you," she said. "I'm surprised at myself because I vowed never to like a Shifter again." She lifted her hand. "But, don't worry, I understand. We're from completely different worlds. When this is over, I'll go back home and read fortunes in the French Quarter, and you'll come make instruments in this workshop until you find a Shifter woman who's your one true mate. I wouldn't mind a postcard from you from time to time, but you'll live your life, and I'll live mine."

Jazz tried to keep up the brave tone and speak matter-of-factly. Her voice faltered on the last words, though, and her aching loneliness scratched at her throat.

Mason laid down the piece of guitar he'd held and came to Jazz. He stopped a foot away from her, just out of reach.

"I told you." His voice was low, filled with anger. "I kissed you because I wanted to. I made love to you because I wanted to. You might have once been with a Feline dirtbag scratching an itch, but I don't pick up and put down females to prove I can. In fact, I—"

Mason broke off, his mouth stiffening, then he jerked himself away and returned to the guitar.

"In fact, what?" Jazz asked. When Mason didn't answer, she marched over to him, positioning herself right behind his strong back. "In fact, *what*? What were you going to say to me?"

Mason swung on her so fast Jazz had to take a step backward. Mason's eyes had gone the light gray of his wolf as he leaned down to her.

"*In fact*, I've never met a woman I wanted to be with as much as I want to be with you. I want to keep on being with you, and knowing you'll go home again, so far away, once we find this fucking healer makes me sick. *In fact*."

"Oh." Jazz's heart began to pound, and she knew he could sense that—a change in her scent, her rising body heat. "You know, they say that you don't really know whether you'll get along with someone until you take a trip together. Then you truly find out whether you like each other. We'll have this trip to find that out."

Mason leaned closer to her. "Yeah? And then what? What do I have to offer you when we come back? I've got nowhere to go but a house with my three brothers, aunt, Broderick's mate, and a couple of strays. *You* live a long way from my Shiftertown in a house with personality. You'll want a better life than Shifter chaos and my pain-in-the-ass brothers, but I hate the thought of you out there by yourself, unprotected and alone. I don't want anything to mess with you, and that includes your dumb-ass house. So what am I supposed to do?"

His anguish was raw. Jazz had seen a similar look in Dale when he'd left her to be with his true mate. He'd been distressed to hurt Jazz, but the quiet happiness in him had been so real that Jazz hadn't had the heart to do anything but kiss his cheek and wish him well.

Mason had the same distress but not the underlying happiness. He was angry, lonely in spite of living in the middle of his big family, and miserable. If his aunt didn't survive it would hurt him profoundly.

Jazz laid her hands on his shoulders and stepped against him. "We'll find the healer," she said softly. "We'll save Aunt Cora. *Then*, we'll talk."

Mason's face softened the slightest bit, though Jazz didn't know whether it was from her promise or her nearness. "I heard that it's never good when women say that," he muttered.

Jazz stopped his words by kissing him. His mouth was hot, more slow goodness, but Jazz sensed Mason's worry and impatience cutting into his burning need.

She slid her arms around him, pulling him closer, letting him know she was there for him, whenever he needed her, for however long.

Jazz knew at that moment, as the kiss grew deeper, that she'd always answer when Mason called, no matter where she was for the rest of her life.

***

The small cargo plane that took them northward was piloted by a thin, weather-beaten man named Marlo who assured Jazz he'd flown all over the world in planes far more rickety than this.

Jazz didn't find this encouraging, and by the look on his face, neither did Mason. But Mason ushered Jazz aboard with his hand on the small of her back, carrying the duffel bag that held clothing and other necessities for them both. Because Jazz hadn't been able to pack anything before she and Mason had fled her house, she'd asked for time to pop into a discount store to buy herself a few tops, a pair of jeans, underwear, and a jacket. Mason had insisted on paying for it all, in cash.

The plane jerked and clanged as it climbed into the sky. Marlo invited them to sit in the front with him, but Mason declined, looking askance at the beat-up chairs in the cockpit. Jazz preferred sitting on the pile of blankets in the back, snuggled up against Mason, in any case.

"Marlo flies Shifters around all over the place," Mason explained, speaking into Jazz's ear over the drone of the engines. "Liam and the other Shiftertown leaders pay him well. He won't betray us."

"Good to know," Jazz said, trying to feel better.

The flight was long, the hours passing tediously. Marlo had to land somewhere in Montana, refueling, and then unhurriedly took them skyward again. Jazz liked the time alone with Mason, the two of them sitting in companionable silence, the engines too loud for them to talk over.

They landed well after dark—where they were, Jazz had no idea.

"We're not far north of Anchorage," Marlo told them as they disembarked into a cool bite of air. "Friend of mine runs things here. Never says a word when I want to come in and out. He's got a pickup you can borrow. As long as you bring it back fueled up, he's not bothered."

"Thanks," Mason said.

"Hey, it's all part of the service."

Marlo waved them off as he shut down the plane, talking jovially to a guy who'd jogged over after they'd landed, neither man paying attention to Jazz and Mason. Mason led Jazz around the hanger to a pickup that had keys dangling from the ignition.

"So," Mason said as he started the truck, Jazz pulling on her jacket in the passenger seat. "Where to?"

"I don't know," Jazz answered blankly. "I've never been to Alaska before." She shivered. "I'm already cold."

Mason's grin flashed in the darkness. "Have you ever been outside Louisiana?"

"Sure," Jazz said at once. "My grandmother and I traveled when I was in high school, driving all the way from New Orleans to Charleston. But we never left the South." She let out a breath. "And I've been to Texas, and now Alaska."

Mason's chuckle rumbled over her. He pulled out, following the only road into the darkness. "Well, now I've been to Louisiana, and Alaska. And Wyoming when I was a kid. That's where we lived before Shifters were outed."

"Are you saying you and I don't get out much?" Jazz asked.

"I'm saying we're out *now*." Mason stepped on the accelerator and the trees on either side of the road began to flow by. "Marlo told me about a motel in town where they won't ask too many questions."

"Nice of him. But *I'll* book the room. I don't want anyone calling the cops if they see your Collar."

Mason agreed, and in the small town they entered, they found a motel that looked remarkably like the one they'd stayed in back in Texas. Jazz went inside to ask for a room—Mason paid, handing Jazz a wad of cash.

Making guitars and music boxes must be lucrative, Jazz decided. She returned with keys—key cards this time—and they moved into the small room at the end of the building.

Jazz thought the long trip might have worn them out too much to make love, but she was wrong. As soon as Mason slid between the sheets with her, his body bare, Jazz came plenty awake. He loved her swiftly, and then more slowly, his touch alternating from gentle to firm and back to caressing. He never closed his eyes, watching her with a steady gaze that held deep passion.

They fell asleep at last, exhausted and spent, Jazz in the curve of Mason's strong arm. At least Jazz was exhausted—she saw the gleam of Mason's eyes in the moonlight as she drifted into pleasant and quiet slumber.

***

In the morning, Mason cranked open the blinds in their room to see blue, clear sky, and a massive mountain rising in the distance.

"Awesome," Jazz said, peering out under his arm. "That's Denali, isn't it? Used to be called Mount McKinley. Tallest mountain in North America. Twenty-thousand feet, or something."

Mason liked her excitement. Jazz seemed able to grab enjoyment out of everything in life. He regarded the snow-capped peak with approval. Mountains, especially prominent ones, were usually sacred spaces, which boded well for their hunt.

His optimism faded after they downed their takeout breakfast and Jazz got started with her psychic search. No matter how much sage smoke choked the room or how many cards Jazz turned over, or how many chants she recited, the stones remained cold, spent, and dormant, no revelation of where the healer was, or if he was even still in this part of Alaska.

"That's what happens sometimes," Jasmine said glumly as the afternoon waned. This far north, the light lingered, but Jasmine's buoyancy flagged. "If a lot of energy courses through the stones, they need to recharge. I hoped enough time would have passed since their last flare, but they probably need to bathe in sunlight and moonlight."

She laid the stones on the windowsill as she spoke, their myriad colors catching the sun and spangling her face. Mason sorted them into patterns in his mind, thinking about an inlay design he'd make, using pieces from stones she loved.

"There's another way to track him," Mason said after she waved her hand over the stones and turned from the window.

"How?" Jasmine's question held skepticism. "Look in the local phonebook for Shifter healers? Ask around for a weird-looking guy with white braids? I'm out of ideas."

"Close," Mason rumbled. "I don't care how much of a loner a Shifter claims to be, all Lupines and Felines need to be around people at some point. Even bears, who enjoy being solitary, need to unwind with friends. A Shifter who lives alone will seek out some kind of company, even if it's human. And a Shifter's favorite habitat away from home is …" He stopped and waited for her to guess.

"Where?" Jasmine asked eagerly.

"A bar."

"Cool." Jasmine shoved her cards together and stuffed them into their bag. "Let me put on something cute, and we'll be off."

Mason scowled. "It's useless for me to argue for you to stay here, isn't it?"

"Yep." Jasmine headed to the bathroom, her hips swaying. "And don't even think about going without me. If you walk into a bar alone, every eye will be focused on you, wondering who you are, and heaven help you if they see your Collar. If I'm with you, all the guys there will be staring at my legs. Or my boobs. You could do a striptease and decorate your Collar with neon lights, and they wouldn't notice."

"Sure," Mason said, and then called as the bathroom door closed, "Not making me feel better!"

***

Turned out that the closest bar to the motel was a little bit out of town down a narrow road. It reminded Mason, when they walked inside, of the roadhouses Mason went to with his brothers that allowed Shifters.

This bar was quieter, with locals who came to have a beer with friends as well as campers and tourists from the nearby national parks. The two groups tended to keep separate, the locals at the bar and the pool tables, the tourists at the small tables in the middle of the room. The tourists talked about the big fish they almost caught; the locals talked about who in town was doing what, or focused their attention on the television.

Mason needed to listen to the locals but he didn't want to push in among them. That would guarantee that they'd shut up or study him too closely, despite Jasmine's claim that all focus would be on her. Mason guided Jasmine to a table on the edge of the tourists' territory, near the pool tables. Jasmine sat down, smiled at the waitress who took their order, and asked for a beer.

The waitress glanced curiously at them when she returned and set bottles in front of them, but with no more curiosity than she would any other out-of-towner. Mason's zipped-up hoodie hid his Collar well, and no one in this chilly part of the world questioned a man keeping his jacket on even inside.

Most men in the bar wore thick shirts with padded vests or light coats. The draft when someone opened the door was chilly.

Jasmine didn't talk much, only sipped her beer and glanced around, fixing her gaze on each man at the pool tables in turn.

Testing their auras, Mason realized. She could sense a Shifter by aura the same way Mason could scent them.

Every once in a while, Jasmine turned to Mason and gave him a little shake of her head. Mason couldn't scent anything either. He supposed they'd have to go into every bar in this part of Alaska and have Mason sniff and Jasmine stare before they found the healer. That should make them popular.

Jasmine's idea that the guys in the bar would mostly be looking at her instead of Mason proved to be true. The problem with that was that Mason's protective instincts woke up and wouldn't climb the hell down.

Every time a man so much as glanced at Jasmine, and especially if that glance lingered, a growl started in Mason's throat. One guy who let his gaze follow the flowering vines of Jasmine's tattoos earned a fierce glare from Mason, and Mason felt his eyes become wolf.

The guy started and turned away quickly. Jasmine slid her hand across the table and rested it on Mason's arm. "Calm down."

"I can't." Mason's voice was guttural. "I don't want them even looking at you."

Jasmine regarded him a moment. "Then maybe we'd better leave."

Mason shook his head. "It will be the same any place we go. And I've decided I don't want you at that motel without me. I'd go crazy worrying about you."

Jasmine looked at him in concern. "So what do we do?"

Mason pressed his hands flat on the table. "I'll control it. I have to. I'll be all right."

Jasmine gave him a doubtful look but started to slide her touch away.

Mason caught her hand. "No. Don't let go of me."

Jasmine stilled a moment, then she closed her fingers around Mason's and held on.

That helped. Mason shut his eyes, willing the wolf in him to quiet.

But the wolf knew his mate. The heat spreading through Mason's heart knew it too. He needed to latch on to Jasmine and not let her go. Not for anything in the world.

They sat there for a time, Jasmine's cool touch the only thing anchoring Mason to his sane self.

It was a tourist, not a local, that finally made Mason snap.

A man in a red plaid shirt, his light brown beard trimmed and combed, his face red from windburn, rose from his chair and sauntered over to their table.

"You don't look like you want to be with him, honey," he said to Jasmine. "You're more than welcome to join us at *our* table."

Jasmine looked up with a smile of *thanks, but no thanks*. All would have been well if the man had shrugged, grinned, and moved back to his friends.

But the man was drunk, and he flushed with anger at Jasmine's brush-off. "Seriously, honey, you can do way better than him. Come on." He put his hand on Jasmine's bare, tattooed arm.

Mason rose in silent fury and launched himself at the man's throat. No warning, no noise, just the killer in him going after a male who dared touch his mate.

The man flailed back in belated alarm. Mason reached for his neck … and found himself blocked by an even larger man whose eyes were pure wolf, his scent, Shifter. The Shifter's black sweatshirt rode down his neck, showing a throat bare and unadorned.

"Not worth it, kid," the Shifter said, a growl edging his voice. "Why don't we go have a drink somewhere else?"

Chapter Twelve

Jazz stared in shock at the man who held Mason back with ease. Well, not exactly ease—his muscles bulged under his sweatshirt as he stood as a solid wall between Mason and his target.

The man was Shifter. His aura screamed it. The psychic cloud around him was much like Mason's but older, more experienced. Mason was sparkling with energy, while this man was more somber. Jazz hadn't sensed him while she was scanning the room—he must have come in just in time to see Mason go for the obnoxious man.

This Shifter wore no Collar, like the man they'd seen in the smoke. But this Shifter and the one in the vision were clearly two different people. The man who held Mason had dark hair, no beard, and light gray eyes. In fact, his eyes were much like Mason's, making Jazz realize he was a Lupine.

"Yes," Jazz said quickly. "Let's go. Come on, Mason."

She got under the new Shifter's arm and touched Mason's shoulder. He moved his gaze to her stiffly, as though he had to force his eyeballs to turn.

Jazz saw that her touch had reached him, though. Mason's jaw unclenched long enough for him to whisper to the other Shifter, "Take me out of here, before I kill him."

"That's right, son," the Shifter said loudly. "We'll go. Tony," he called to the bartender. "Give these guys a round and put it on my tab."

Tony must have known the Shifter well, because he only nodded and started setting up beer bottles.

The man who'd propositioned Jazz looked unhappy but his friends yelled at him to give up and sit down. He didn't have a chance with someone like her, they said — she was way out of his league.

Jazz carefully didn't look at any of them as she took up her jacket and walked close beside Mason and the other Shifter past the tables and out of the bar.

Once they'd reached the far end of the parking lot, Mason jerked free of the other Shifter.

"Who the hell are you?" Mason put himself directly in front of Jazz so the Shifter would have to go around him to get anywhere near her.

"Calm yourself," the older Shifter said irritably. "Could you have tried to broadcast any louder that you're Shifter? A long way from home too?" He flicked his hand at Mason's neck where his Collar now peeped over his half-unzipped jacket.

Mason's gaze went to the other man's neck, which had no Collar at all. "Rogue," he said with a snarl.

"No, not a rogue," the Shifter said in a low voice. "My dad and I just didn't feel like getting rounded up twenty years ago. I'm Ezra. Who are you?"

"Mason," Mason said between his teeth. "From Austin."

"Ah." Ezra nodded as though something made sense. "She's human." He jerked his chin at Jazz.

"Yes, I am," Jazz said around Mason. "And standing right here. I'm Jasmine. From New Orleans."

"Moncrieff sent me," Ezra said, looking at her with a stare as piercing as Mason's.

"Who's Moncrieff?" Jazz asked, as Mason seemed unable to speak.

Ezra frowned. "He said you were looking for him. I was supposed to find you and give you directions."

"Well, why didn't you say so?" Jazz squirmed around Mason, who stood like a monolith. "How did he know we were coming?"

Ezra shook his head. "No idea. He just said that a Lupine and a pretty human woman with black hair and flowers on her arm would be up here sooner or later, and would probably land at the old airstrip. So I've been hanging out in bars waiting for you to show up instead of being comfortable at home."

Mason drew a breath, and when he spoke, his voice was forced. "And we thank you. So, where is he?"

The directions were complicated. Ezra instructed them to drive down the highway that led out of town to a turnoff, four miles along that road to the west to another turnoff, then another tiny road when they reached the lake, then they had to walk a mile after that. GPS, Ezra said, wasn't reliable to find it, so Jazz wrote the directions down in the little notebook she'd brought with her.

"Might be easier if you drove us," Jazz suggested. She tried a winsome smile, but this seemed to be lost on Ezra.

"I'm not going anywhere near Moncrieff if I can help it," Ezra answered. "You'll be fine," he said to Mason, "as long as that Collar hasn't messed up your sense of smell."

Mason growled at him, but he was calmer now, his voice steadier. "It hasn't," he said. He hesitated. "Thank you."

Ezra snorted a laugh. "Don't thank me until you meet Moncrieff. Goddess go with you." He turned away, walking briskly toward the trees beyond the parking lot. "Oh, one more thing," Ezra said, pausing to look back. "Moncrieff is totally insane."

He swung away and walked off into the darkness, his boots crunching on rocks then fading as he vanished from sight.

***

Mason drove down the empty highway while Jasmine sat next to him and read the directions out of her notebook, lit by a tiny flashlight. Mason could have told her she didn't need to bother; he remembered exactly what Ezra had said, but he didn't have the heart. She was enjoying herself.

Excitement put pink into her cheeks, a sparkle in her eyes. Her lips curved, and when she peered down the road, the pucker between her brows was cute.

Mason knew damn well he'd never have made it this far without her. Before he'd met her, he'd thought psychics were simply scam artists or at least seriously deluded, but Jasmine seemed to have real abilities. He couldn't deny that the glowing stones had pointed the way and that she'd conjured the image of the healer in her sage smoke.

Now she was animated with interest, ready for the end of the quest, both to satisfy her curiosity and because of genuine concern for Aunt Cora and the feral Shifter — people she'd only just met.

When it was over, when — *if* the healer could help — Jasmine would return to her life in her house outside New Orleans, and Mason would go home to Shiftertown.

No, the wolf inside him said sternly. *Don't let her go.*

In the old days, a Shifter could snatch up the female he wanted, run off with her into the wild, and hole up with her in mating frenzy until a cub came along. It had been a perfectly acceptable form of courtship, because females had been scarce, plus if a male didn't hide his mate, she might be stolen from him.

In these more civilized days, the male made a mate-claim, allowed the female to choose whether to accept or refuse, and he politely didn't lock her in a basement and have sex with her for days — unless she wanted him to, of course. Mason wasn't certain what Jasmine would say to an invitation to cohabit Mason's basement. The wolf in him wanted to say to hell with it and invoke the old ways, but Mason was pretty sure his brothers, Liam, and the human police might object, even if Jasmine didn't.

Even so, Mason wouldn't let her go so easily. There were ways ...

Mason set his teeth, willing his wolf to shut up. They still had to find the bloody healer.

Ezra's directions were good. Jasmine pointed eagerly when she saw the last turnoff, and Mason drove to the end of the road by the lake, and parked.

Mason took the keys with him as he locked the pickup. He didn't suggest Jasmine stay there and not attempt what might be an arduous hike through the woods, because Mason didn't want her out of his sight. The thought of Jasmine sitting alone in the truck, visible to any human predator who might happen along, made his blood cold.

The trail through the woods was fairly rough, though Mason hadn't expected anything else. When a Shifter wanted to hide himself, he could do it thoroughly. Mason tugged branches out of the way and held Jasmine steady as they picked their way along.

Jasmine used her flashlight to keep from tripping, but Mason instructed her to keep it low so it wouldn't night blind him. His Shifter vision lit the way far better for him than a flashlight ever could.

At long last, they came into a clearing in the thin trees, the sky spreading above them. It was breathtaking, that sky, with every star the lights of the cities hid standing out in perfect clarity. Mason swore he could see to forever standing out here.

Under this sparkling beauty lay a trailer house, long, narrow, and weather-beaten, its foundation and roof rusty from snow, rain, and overall dampness.

Jasmine snapped off her flashlight and cocked her head at the trailer. "He's in there," she whispered.

Mason knew he was too. He'd caught the faint scent that meant Shifter, and Jasmine was staring at the wall by the front door as though she could see his aura through it.

A very faint glow lit up one of the windows, barely discernible behind whatever shade was pulled down. The healer was there, and he was watching television.

The mundane sight of the TV's light made Mason's rage boil over. Aunt Cora was lying in bed, torn up, possibly dying, while this asshole who could make her better in a second was hiding out here watching whatever the big satellite dish on top of his trailer picked up.

Mason told Jasmine to stay put until he signaled to her, then he strode across the clearing without bothering to be quiet. He climbed the flimsy steps to the equally flimsy porch and banged on the door with both fists.

The television went off. All was silent, no more light from within. Mason wondered if the guy had dived out a back window or had an escape hatch in the floor. If he did, Mason was going after him and dragging him back.

Then Mason heard the sound of heavy feet inside, a stride that vibrated the entire trailer and its porch. The door in front of Mason was suddenly wrenched open so hard that Mason was surprised it stayed on its hinges.

"What?"

The man who bellowed the word was big. Very big. Fucking huge. Mason found his head going back trying to take him in.

Two thin white braids with blue beads woven into them hung on either side of the man's large face, and the rest of his hair was the same white, cut very short, but he wasn't elderly. His hair was white-blond, like a Norseman's, and the beard that framed his mouth was jet black.

His eyes were just as black, glittering and intense. Mason had seen eyes like his before—not just in the vision but on someone else, though at the moment, he couldn't remember who.

The man was a giant, packed solidly with muscle under a black T-shirt, blue jeans, and a black duster coat that flapped around his calves. Mason stared at him, realizing with a jolt that it might not be as easy to hog-tie him and drag him off as Mason hoped.

Didn't matter. If Mason had to fight this guy to make him come to Austin, then he had to fight him. Mason was desperate. He'd win.

Behind him, Jasmine started across the clearing. "Are you Moncrieff?" she called. "The healer?"

The big man stepped out onto the porch, nearly knocking Mason aside. He was barefoot, despite his duster, but he didn't seem to notice. "No!" he yelled at Jasmine.

"I know you are," Jasmine said impatiently. "We need your hel—"

Her word cut off into a shriek as she disappeared from sight. Mason was off the porch in an instant, never feeling his feet move as he sprinted to her.

Mason found her lying flat on the wet grass in the middle of the clearing, fighting a net that had fallen on top of her. Mason realized that the healer hadn't shouted *No!* to deny he was Moncrieff, but to stop

Jasmine running across the clearing into his booby trap.

Moncrieff had charged after Mason at a surprisingly rapid pace and reached Jasmine a few steps behind him. They both grabbed for the net and started untangling Jasmine.

Mason glared at the Shifter. "What kind of asshole lays traps in front of his own house? If you've hurt her, I'm ripping out your throat."

Mason's Collar sparked, right over the patch of throat that corresponded to the one he'd tear out of Moncrieff, but Mason barely felt the sting.

"It's just a net to scare off trespassers," Moncrieff said, his voice a very deep rumble. "Nothing deadly."

"Mason, I'm all right," Jasmine said under the mass of cords. "Really."

"I don't hurt people." Moncrieff lifted away enough of the net to free Jasmine. He held a broad hand out to her. "I'm a *healer*, dick-brain. I heal. Okay, so I wouldn't hurt anyone *much*. You all right, sweetheart?"

Mason nearly body-slammed Moncrieff out of the way before the man could touch Jasmine. Mason seized Jasmine's hand himself and helped her to her feet.

He saw that Jasmine had tripped over a simple rope that had sent her to the ground at the same time it had released the net from where it had hung in a tree. The net was cloth, more like one for home tennis or volleyball games than anything from an over-the-top security store. Mason hadn't triggered it when he'd crossed the clearing—the Shifter part of him must have sensed and skirted the trap while he'd been intent on rushing the house and dragging out Moncrieff.

"Follow me," Moncrieff said sternly to Mason. "Right where I walk, nowhere else. Got it?"

He glared at Mason, not Jasmine, then swung around and led the way to the house.

They reached the trailer without further mishap. The house inside was as narrow as the outside made it look, and it was a mess. Pots and pans cluttered the tiny kitchen—all clean, not used—and junk lay everywhere. Books, magazines, coils of fishing line, DVDs, clothes, blankets, towels, clay bowls, stones like the ones Jasmine used, empty beer cans, a pile of boots .... There was a relatively clean space on the sofa where Moncrieff obviously reclined while he was watching the large flat-screen TV in the opposite corner.

Jasmine walked in, not waiting for Mason's okay. "You *are* Moncrieff, aren't you?" she asked the big man.

His braids swung as he jerked around to her. "Who wants to know?"

"You told Ezra to look for us and send us to you." Jasmine met his eyes without worry. "So you must already know who we are."

Moncrieff flicked his very black gaze to Mason, his lips twitching. "I like her. Yeah, I saw you in the smoke, sweetheart, but I don't know who you are. The Goddess seemed strong in you, so I knew you'd find your way up here sooner or later. I know the guy who owns the airstrip, and knew what motel he'd send you to. I guessed you'd start looking for me by listening to bar gossip, and I told Ezra to go to the bars closest to your motel and wait for you to show up. But I don't know who you *are*. Why don't you tell me, honey, before I toss *him* out the back door and invite you to share my warmed-up pizza?"

Mason's growl began to fill the trailer as Moncrieff spoke, growing louder when he finished. Moncrieff growled right back at him, his rumble topping Mason's. The loose dishes on the counter began to rattle.

"Will you two *stop*?" Jasmine clapped her hands over her ears. "This place will fall down. There's no mystery. I'm Jasmine Samuelson from New Orleans, and he's Mason McNaughton from Austin. You need to come with us and heal Mason's aunt before she dies, and a feral Shifter."

Moncrieff stopped, the noise dying. He fixed his eyes on Mason again, a faint red glow appearing among the black. "A feral? Are you shitting me?"

Mason shook his head. "I wish I was. He's going to gut my family one by one if he's not stopped."

Moncrieff's voice was hard. "Just kill the bastard and put him out of his misery."

"He's got a cub on the way," Mason countered. "Aleck's a good guy … Okay, so I've never really liked him, but his mate loves him, and my brother's mate is Aleck's mate's sister—got all that? I have to live in the same house with them, and my aunt's about to die because Aleck tore her up. So I'm here to haul your ass to Austin to fix all this."

Moncrieff stared at him. Mason realized he was babbling, distraught, furious, and already grieving for Aunt Cora. If she died, Mason would kill Aleck and then this Moncrieff guy himself.

Moncrieff's gaze filled with cold harshness as he lifted his hand and pointed at the door.

"Out. Now. I should have shoved you under the net with her, no matter how cute she is. No one can heal a feral, kid. Forget it."

This was Moncrieff's territory, as full of junk as it was. The invisible boundaries that encompassed the area he was lord and master of extended from the trailer and over a wide distance around it. All the way to the road, Mason had sensed. Moncrieff was dominant here, and what he said was law. If he told Mason to go, Mason had to go. His instincts would force him to even if Moncrieff didn't bodily throw him out.

Mason dug in his heels, willing those instincts to stay down. At home, he was used to doing whatever his brothers told him, but Mason knew he wasn't entirely without dominance. He might be the end of the line in his own house, but compared to other Shifters, he was not all that far down in the hierarchy.

He squared his shoulders and looked Moncrieff right in the eye.

He knew in that instant that Moncrieff was more alpha than anyone Mason had ever met except maybe for Dylan Morrissey. Even Broderick backed down from Dylan when he had to. The only person Moncrieff might concede dominance to was Tiger.

Why the *hell* had Tiger insisted Mason and Jasmine come up here alone? Tiger would have had the man halfway to Marlo's plane by now.

You will succeed, and bring back the healer, Tiger had said.

Mason lifted his chin, ready to fight. Moncrieff gave him another warning growl. Mason had no idea what kind of creature this guy turned into, and it couldn't be good, but it didn't matter.

"Stop it!" Jasmine stepped right between them — was she nuts? She held up her hands, one toward each of them. "This isn't helping. Mr. Moncrieff, we *need* you. I have no idea what it takes to heal a Shifter who is going feral, but can you at least *try*? And help Mason's aunt. None of this is her fault."

"Sweetheart, there's a reason I hide out in the woods," Moncrieff began, but Jasmine thrust her palm against him.

Mason stiffened as Moncrieff's eyes widened in astonishment. Mason was sure Moncrieff would simply toss Jasmine aside — and then Mason would fight him and likely lose. But the man only stood there.

"I'm not finished," Jasmine said to him. "Shifters need you. Cutting yourself off from them doesn't make any sense. It took a hell of a lot of effort and energy for us to find you, let alone travel up here after you. The least you can do is come back with us and see if you can help. What is *wrong* with you?"

Moncrieff stared at her. Mason stood poised, waiting to attack if Moncrieff so much as touched her, but the man only regarded Jasmine with enigmatic eyes.

"You'd be amazed at what's wrong with me, sweetie," he said, his voice quiet. "Truly amazed."

Jasmine didn't move. "So, will you come with us, Mr. Moncrieff?"

Or will I have to fight you and kill myself trying? Mason continued silently.

The big man kept his gaze on Jasmine for a long time. His chest rose and fell with each breath, the

Shifter in him unhappy. Mason also scented something in him almost like fear. *Fear of what?*

Moncrieff switched his gaze back to Mason. Yep, this guy was deathly afraid of something. Moncrieff kept staring at him, and Mason stared right back.

Finally the man closed his eyes, tipped his head back, and let out a sound that was both growl and grunt. "All right! I'll do it. Probably the stupidest thing I'll ever do in my life, but what the hell?" He looked at Jasmine again, totally ignoring Mason. "But only if you do two things for *me*, honey."

Chapter Thirteen

"What?" Jasmine asked. She removed her hand from the man's chest and waited expectantly.

"First, stop calling me Mr. Moncrieff."

Jasmine pursed her lips in surprise. "Isn't that your name?"

"It is, but only part of it." He drew himself up. "My full name is Alexander Johansson Moncrieff. But my friends call me Zander."

"All right," Jasmine said brightly. "Zander then. What's the other thing you want?"

Zander broke into a sudden grin. "There are some hunters up here trying to stalk and kill a wild grizzly, and it's pissing me off." His eyes lost their fear and took up a mad sparkle as he finally looked again at Mason. "Help me scare the shit out of them, kid, and then I'll go with you."

***

Fifteen minutes later, Mason understood Ezra's warning that Zander Moncrieff was totally insane.

Mason followed the man through the trees on silent feet, both of them naked. Zander had insisted they shuck their clothes before they left, so they could shift at a moment's notice. Made sense, but the underbrush was slashing the hell out of Mason's unprotected feet and legs. When he'd asked why they didn't just shift first, Zander had shaken his head.

"If they see anything four-legged in the trees, they'll simply shoot it," Zander had said. "Don't shift until I give you the signal."

Mason had understood his point—if the hunters were that happy to kill, they'd have to be careful.

Jasmine had stayed behind without argument. Without *much* argument, Mason amended. She'd seen the sense in her not going up against hunters with guns. She hadn't let Mason go, though, before she'd lit a sage stick and waved smoke all over him, while Zander had watched, amused.

The hunters had set up camp a few miles from Zander's house. They weren't hiding—Mason smelled their campfire and whatever they'd cooked, and the glow of their fire lit the night. They didn't fear anything out here, the idiots.

Zander, Mason had to admit, was good at stealth. He moved quickly and silently despite his size, running over ground with athletic ease. Mason came behind, striving to keep up with the bigger man, shadows swallowing both of them.

Zander didn't wait to plot his strategy or share with Mason what he planned to do. He simply shifted to half man, half beast without warning and sprinted toward the camp.

When Mason saw the form of Zander's half-shifted state, he understood why he hadn't figured out Zander's animal. He was a bear—but not just any bear.

The fur that caught the starlight as Zander rose was pure white, his paws and tip of his long muzzle black. Not that Mason could see much of his nose, because Zander's fangs gleamed as he let out a roar.

Mason knew now where he'd seen eyes that black—Olaf, the polar bear cub who lived down the street in the Austin Shiftertown had eyes exactly like Zander's.

But while Olaf, when he was half shifted to polar bear and roaring, was adorable, Zander Moncrieff was terrifying.

The men in the camp dropped whatever they were drinking and scrambled up as Zander raised his arms and came at them.

"Fucking hell!" one of them yelled. "It's a yeti. I swear to God."

Most Shifters figured that what humans called a yeti was in truth a Shifter. Probably Zander, Mason thought now, messing with their minds.

Zander roared again, a menacing hulk just outside the light of their campfires. The hunters grabbed shotguns and started shooting, but Zander dropped and moved so fast they never got a bead on him.

Goddess, he seriously *was* insane, Mason snarled silently. Zander wasn't that far from the hunters, and at some point, one of them would hit him. Then Mason would have a shot-up healer on his hands, which wouldn't do Aunt Cora any good.

Mason shifted all the way to wolf and dashed into the camp. Everyone was looking at Zander, so

Mason ran in without anyone seeing him and started knocking over tents. When a few men turned back at the commotion, Mason barreled into them, too close for their aim. Guns dropped from hands. Mason shifted to his half beast long enough to scoop up the weapons and run off with them.

He dumped the shotguns in the woods then shifted to full wolf and sprinted back for more while Zander distracted them by playing yeti. Soon, five of the half dozen hunters were shotgun-less, while the sixth aimed wildly at Zander.

Zander lifted one of the guns Mason had liberated, waved it in the air, and then broke it apart between his massive hands.

The sixth hunter aimed right at him. Zander made a perfect target silhouetted against the starlight, and he had no time to duck. Mason slammed himself into the hunter, and the gun went off, the shot going wide.

Zander hit the ground but came up with another shotgun, roaring like a movie monster as he ripped it to pieces. *Fucking show-off.*

The hunters ran, careening into each other as they sprinted for the SUVs at the edge of the clearing. Zander stomped on another of the guns, then he roared again, his muzzle reaching for the sky.

When he came down, he landed on all fours as full bear—the most gigantic polar bear Mason had ever seen. Not that he'd ever seen a polar bear up close before, besides Olaf, and Olaf was a cute little cub.

There was nothing cute about Zander. He charged after the hunters, no playing around now. He thundered over the brush and through the trees, his coat a flash of white, his gaping mouth red and savage.

The hunters shouted, screamed, and flung themselves into the two vehicles at the edge of the trees. One of the SUVs didn't want to start, and the men inside it gibbered as Zander slammed his full bodyweight into it. He rocked the SUV back and forth, the men yelling and urging the driver to get them the fuck out of there.

The first SUV didn't wait for them. It leapt away in a cloud of dust, red lights flashing while their friends cried out, alternately swearing and praying at the tops of their voices. Zander, rising to his half beast again, brought his fists down on the SUV's back window, shattering it just as the vehicle roared to life.

The driver stomped on the gas, and the SUV leapt away, skidding on dirt and mud before it righted itself and shot after the first one. Mason found himself bathed in a wash of exhaust, left alone with a twinkling campfire, a pile of broken guns, wrecked tents, and a seriously crazy polar bear.

Zander shifted to human and burst into wild laughter. "Assholes!" he yelled. "Woo-hoo! Look at 'em run."

Mason shook himself and shifted back to human. "Are you stupid?" he snarled at Zander. "It's funny now, but what happens when they stop being scared and start getting mad? If they report that a bear and a wolf tried to kill them, they'll have all kinds of hunters, park rangers, and whoever else out here to round us up and take us down. Goddess help us if they figure out we're Shifters."

Zander stopped laughing, his exuberance dying as though he'd flipped a switch. "Good point. I guess we'd better go."

Without another word Zander turned, shifted to bear, and started at a dead run back toward the trailer.

This is for Aunt Cora, Mason told himself as he shifted to wolf and ran after Zander. He had to repeat that several times and grit his teeth until he tasted blood. Otherwise he'd strangle the idiot before they got him home.

***

Zander sat in the copilot's seat on the way to Austin, while Jazz and Mason again rode in the back. Mason had been tightlipped about the raid on the hunters' camp, but Zander had gloated.

"You should have seen it, sweetie," Zander had said as he'd burst back into the house and grabbed a pair of jeans. Jazz had quickly averted her eyes, turning around until she was certain Zander had covered his very large body. "Mason and me had them running like their asses were on fire."

"Let's just go," Mason had snapped, reaching for his own clothes. Jazz didn't bother to look away from *him.* He was all growly and irritated, which made him cute, though Jazz would never tell him so.

Now she and Mason sat shoulder to shoulder, bumping against each other when the plane jolted with turbulence. Mason was staring at the back of Zander's chair as Zander talked enthusiastically with Marlo.

"He's afraid," Mason said.

Jazz was startled at the declaration, but then she studied Zander, who'd resumed his clothes and duster coat.

He had an intriguing aura, silver-gray shot through with white, which matched his white hair and black eyes, as though everything about him had to be monochrome. Zander had an especially strong spiritual connection with the Goddess, Jazz sensed, one that not even other Shifters had.

"Interesting," Jazz said. "Afraid of what? The feral Shifter? I know Aleck is dangerous, but even your aunt stood up to him."

Mason shook his head. "I don't think it's fear of physical pain or having to fight. I saw Zander go after those hunters—he stood up in front of gunfire without flinching. He wasn't trying to hurt the guys; he just wanted to scare them, but he wasn't afraid of taking on a group of armed humans. No, there's something else going on with him."

"Yeah, he's hard to read," Jazz said. She slid her hand over Mason's, liking how he instantly closed his fingers around hers. "I've been thinking about something," she went on. "When I came downstairs at the safe house and found the stones blazing and the amber lighting you up … Mason, it wasn't *my* psychic ability that put the final piece of the puzzle together. It was *yours*."

Mason's brows drew together. "What the hell are you talking about? I'm not psychic."

"Not necessarily psychic, per se," Jazz said, tracing a line on his palm. "But you're more attuned to the metaphysical side of life than you know. Amber in particular reacts to latent power, because it's so ancient. It used to be tree resin—part of a living thing."

Mason shrugged, uncomfortable. "The stones must have had whatever residual woo-woo stuff you did to them at the motel inside them. It was you, not me."

"Don't think so." Jazz liked touching his hands. They held such strength, yet these broad fingers had so precisely fashioned the inlay on his music box. "The stones were pretty spent, as I said. I couldn't get anything out of them at all. But you did."

"Whatever happened, it wasn't me," Mason said impatiently. "I'm not—"

"Goddess-touched," a big voice rumbled.

Jazz jerked her head up to see Zander standing over them, his white braids swinging as he reached into the cooler next to Jazz and brought out a dripping can of soda.

"What are you talking about?" Mason asked him, irritated.

"Goddess-touched," Zander repeated. "Means the magic of the Goddess runs strong in you. Probably through your whole clan."

Jazz squeezed Mason's hand. "That makes total sense," she said excitedly to him. "You said your family had Guardian ancestry and that your brother could use a Guardian's sword. You bonded with my house real quick, and you really did charge the stones so they could find Zander."

"Yep." Zander gave her a nod. Jazz saw the haunted look in Zander's eyes as he leaned down again to grab a bag of chips from a box that constituted what Marlo called *in-flight dining.* "Definitely Goddess-touched," Zander said as he turned away. He tossed over his shoulder, "Takes one to know one."

Mason only muttered, "Don't tell me I have to be like him. *Please.*"

Jazz watched Zander slide into the seat in the cockpit, rip open the bag of chips, then laugh uproariously at something Marlo said before pouring half the contents of the bag into his mouth.

"No." Jazz leaned her head against Mason's shoulder. "I think you're fine the way you are."

***

Zander continued to be a total pain in the ass all the way from the airstrip out in the middle of nowhere Texas into Austin. Dylan came to pick them up, and Mason had to wonder why. Dylan didn't run errands.

Mason realized as the miles went by and Austin appeared on the horizon that Dylan had come to check out Zander. Zander had no Collar, didn't come from a Shiftertown, and lived on his own without any clan that Mason had been able to discern. The man's trailer hadn't had any photos or other personal mementos of family on its walls.

Alone and clanless. Mason shuddered. He couldn't imagine that. He drew Jasmine closer, clamping down on his need to do nothing but kiss her as they rode in through Austin and made for Shiftertown.

They reached home at about nine in the morning. The sun was up, the air cool and dry—a beautiful day for Austin. When Dylan stopped the truck in front of Mason's house, Mason knew immediately that they might have come too late.

Aleck's roar boomed from the basement, and Mason heard banging on a small barred window in the house's foundation. If Aleck found a way to break free, anyone in Shiftertown would be fair game. He could kill plenty of cubs before they got him tranqued.

Zander's face drained of color as he emerged from the pickup, his eyes going bleak. Terror. Mason exchanged a glance with Jasmine, and she nodded.

"Let me see your auntie first," Zander said, heading for the house. "She in here too?"

Mason watched for a surprised moment as Zander strode rapidly through the yard and on up to the porch, his duster coat swirling around him. The man was about to open the door and walk right into another Shifter's home—Mason's brothers would disembowel him.

Mason sprinted after him. He made it onto the porch as Zander reached for the doorknob, and he shoved himself in Zander's way.

"Are you insane?" Mason demanded. He pushed open the door and walked into the house first. Sure enough, his brothers Corey and Derek were pouring down the stairs, eyes flat, ready to fight the intruder. "You don't just barge into another Shifter's territory," Mason said angrily. "I'm surprised you're still alive."

"I'm a healer," Zander replied without inflection. "We have different rules."

"That just means you haven't met Broderick." Mason looked around. "Where is he, by the way?" he asked his brothers, who'd halted but looked mad as hell.

"Downstairs, trying to keep Aleck in," Corey answered with a grunt. He gave Zander a once-over, obviously not liking what he saw. "We built a big cage in one of the rooms, welded the bars ourselves. Aleck's been trying to tear it apart. When he's coherent, he claims we're trying to keep him from his mate and cub."

"Well, we are," Mason said impatiently. "This is Zander Moncrieff. He wants to see Aunt Cora."

"Joanne and Nancy are with her," Corey said, arms folded. Derek, the brother closest to Mason in age, said nothing, but his anger was palpable.

Zander let Mason lead the way up the stairs and didn't try to push past him. Jasmine came right behind Mason, and Mason reached back and clasped her hand. He felt better holding on to her.

Aunt Cora was not doing well. Mason's chest burned when he saw her, her face sunken and wan, her usual vitality absent. Aunt Cora had the silk scarf he'd bought her draped loosely around her shoulders, and she tried to focus on Mason as he came in. Mason saw in her eyes that she knew she was dying.

"Don't look so horrified," Aunt Cora said, her voice a weak scratch. "Does nothing for my ego. I'm glad to see you and Jasmine made it home. And what is *that*?" She glared up at Zander.

As Mason watched, Zander underwent a transformation. The overly loud Shifter forcing joviality to hide his anger and fear vanished, and a man filled with compassion took his place. Zander's dark eyes softened as he sank down next to the bed and took Aunt Cora's wasted hand.

"I'm Zander Moncrieff," he said. "Of the Shetland Island Moncrieffs. I'm here to heal you."

Aunt Cora regarded him with deep suspicion. "Are you? Or is the whole Shifter mystical healer thing a bunch of bullshit?"

Zander very gently squeezed her hand. "It's all true. Unfortunately." He brushed his finger over her forehead and rose. "Mason—talk to you in the hall?"

The fact that he asked *Mason* to have a consultation outside the room, not Corey or Derek, nor did he ask for Broderick, stunned everyone, including Aunt Cora. Nancy and Joanne, who sat very close together on a sofa, Joanne's arm linked with Nancy's, both watched with interest, startled out of their worries. Derek looked enraged; Corey bemused.

Zander paid no attention to their reaction as Mason and Jasmine followed Zander into the wide, square hall. Zander leaned down and spoke to them in a quiet voice.

"Here's what you need to know about healers, Mason. I can heal your aunt. It will be tough but I can do it." Zander's look was somber. "What happens, though, after I heal a Shifter is that *they* are fine, but I'm not. The Goddess played a bloody good joke on me. I can heal, but only if I then take on all the pain and suffering of the person I've just saved. Not the actual wounds or illness—but I experience the same pain. I don't know how it works, but it doesn't really matter. It lays me out for a long time— sometimes days. Once it was a couple of weeks before I recovered. That's why I live alone, my friends. I have to recharge before I can possibly help anyone else. The thing is ..." Zander paused and ran his finger across his chin. "If I heal your aunt, I know I'll be too spent to heal the feral, and it sounds like you either have to help him or put him down, very, very soon. I might not recover in time to do anything for him. I've never tried healing a feral before, so who the hell knows what I'll be like after that? I might not come out of it at all, and then you'll have an insane polar bear on your hands." He let out a breath, his lips bloodless.

"So you need to choose, kid," Zander finished, midnight-dark eyes on Mason. "Do you want me to heal your aunt, or the feral? Because I doubt I can do both."

Chapter Fourteen

Mason answered at once. "There is no choice. Aunt Cora."

"I don't think so." Aunt Cora's wavering voice came from inside the room. "I can hear you, Mason. I'm not gone yet."

Mason dropped Jasmine's hand and pushed past Zander into the bedroom, barely able to breathe through his anger. He sensed Jasmine behind him — he'd always know when she was near.

"It has to be you, auntie," Mason said with conviction. "Aleck's already gone. If you could hear me in the hall, then you can hear Aleck in the basement." He swung on Zander and demanded, "Why didn't you tell me this before?"

Zander's expression was grim. "I couldn't be sure until I saw how badly your aunt was hurt, and how feral your friend is."

"Which means he thinks I'm seriously hurt," Aunt Cora said. "I agree. Look over there, Mason." She pointed to where Nancy and Joanne listened, stunned. "Nancy will soon have a cub. That cub needs its dad. Aleck and his little family are just beginning in life, while I've lived a good, long time. I'm not in a hurry to go, but if there's a chance to save Aleck, I say take it."

"No," Mason said, resolute. His two brothers filled the doorway, and he knew their opinion was solidly with his. Only Broderick was absent, but Mason knew Broderick would agree that Aunt Cora came first.

Jasmine had moved across the room to stand with Nancy and Joanne. She looked worried, uncertain, but she said softly, "I think it's up to your aunt, Mason."

"No," Mason repeated. Letting Aunt Cora go was not an option. The crazed beast in the basement was already a long way gone, and who knew if Zander could do anything for him after all? Zander was afraid he couldn't. If Zander spent himself, as he claimed, in a futile attempt to save Aleck, they'd lose both Aleck *and* Aunt Cora.

Derek and Corey growled behind Mason, a wall of accord.

"Mason ..." Aunt Cora began.

"Your aunt is right," Zander said. "It's not up to you to choose who gets healed and who doesn't. It's the choice of the heal-ee."

"And I say, go save Aleck," Aunt Cora said, her tone decided. "Let the cub have a father. Then if you have anything left, healer, come back and see me."

She pressed her lips together and closed her eyes, argument over.

Nancy said nothing at all. She was crying silently, knowing that Mason and his family had never wanted anything to do with her and Aleck. Broderick had brought Aleck and Nancy here because they'd had nowhere else to go, and Broderick had wanted to please Joanne. Joanne knew it, and looked distressed and unhappy. The two women had come to love Aunt Cora in their own right.

Zander started to leave the room only to find his way blocked by Mason, Derek, and Corey. He stopped, his expression holding sorrow but also determination.

"It's her choice, Mason," Zander said.

"Do you honestly think you can bring Aleck back?" Mason asked him. "And do it without it messing yourself up too much to heal her?"

"No," Zander said, truth in his voice. "This might kill me. But I have to do it. It's what the Goddess chose me for."

Mason's heart pounded. He faced down Zander, who continued to simply look at him. Could a giant polar bear best three furious wolves? Looked like they were about to find out.

"Mason, let him," Jasmine's clear voice cut into his jumbled thoughts, and then her cool presence was next to him, her touch on his hand. "Let him try. I'll be there—I can help."

Before Mason could snarl that he wasn't about to let Jasmine anywhere near the crazy Shifter in the basement, Zander said, "You too, Mason. Both of you can ground me and keep me from going insane. You're both Goddess-touched. It's the best chance we have."

"Shit," Mason said. His throat was tight and aching, his wolf wanting to knock Zander to the floor until Zander agreed to try first with Aunt Cora. Only Jasmine's touch pulled him back from his frenzy.

"All right, all right." Mason glared at Zander. "But the minute you know you can't save him, I'm hauling your ass out of there and bringing you back to Aunt Cora."

Zander nodded. "Sounds reasonable." He started out the door, pushing Derek and Corey aside without any effort at all. Mason guessed he knew who would have lost that fight.

***

Jazz grew colder as Mason opened the door to the basement and led her and Zander down the stairs. Not only was the air cooler, but an aura of fear and rage blanketed everything. She shivered and drew closer to Mason.

She clutched her bag of accoutrements and wondered how her innocent crystals and stones could make a dent in the crazed anger that flowed over the basement. She had sensed some of Aleck's insanity upstairs, but here it was so thick and dense she felt as though she walked through fetid swamp water.

The main room of the basement was mostly storage, overflow from the house above. In one corner, someone had set up a small television and a couple of comfortable chairs.

The back part of the basement had been partitioned off with a wall and one door. Behind it was Aleck.

Jasmine knew he was there before Broderick, who'd met them at the bottom of the stairs, a tranq rifle over his shoulder, unlocked and opened the door. Aleck's red and black aura had hit her as soon as she'd stepped into the main basement, no wall able to keep it contained. The door itself was flimsy, a cheap one from a hardware store with a standard lock, but that wasn't what held the feral in.

Bars had been built across the long and narrow room they entered. Two inches thick, the bars had been embedded into the cement walls and floor and drilled through the ceiling above. The welding job was expert, Broderick and his brothers able to build more than music boxes.

Jazz knew the bars were strong, because when Aleck slammed himself into them from across the room, they didn't move.

As soon as she looked at Aleck, she realized why Mason was now convinced that Zander could do nothing for him. Aleck had shifted so that he was half man, half Feline. From the markings, Jazz guessed leopard, though it was hard to tell. His face was mostly eyes and fangs, the need to kill high as he fixed on Mason and Broderick.

Whatever had been sane in this Shifter was gone. Spittle ran down his face and into his fur, and the hands that held the bars had broken and ragged claws.

Zander walked into the room and right up to the bars. Aleck switched his gaze to Zander, and his eyes filmed with red, his fury growing. Zander took him in and said, "Well, that's not good."

"Too far gone?" Mason asked, sounding a little more hopeful. "All right, tranq him Brod, and we'll go help Aunt Cora."

"I *did* tranq him," Broderick replied with his usual gruffness. "You should have seen him before you came down here."

"Then I guess Zander can't help him." Mason jerked a thumb at the larger man. "That's him, by the way, the healer."

"I figured." Broderick pinned Zander with a stare. "I felt him come in, violating my territory. You're bear, Mason told me on the phone. Figures. All bears are arrogant shitheads. Think you can do anything for Aleck?" he asked Zander, no apology in his tone.

Zander hadn't taken his eyes off Aleck. "Yes," he said quietly. "But I'll need to get in there with him."

Mason put out a quick hand. "If you go in there, he'll kill you."

"No, he won't." Zander's voice was quiet but held determination. "Jazz, sweetie, take out your strongest stones and spread them outside the base of the cage, close to the bars. Ask the Goddess to fill them with everything she's got. Then sage the place up. A nice cloud of it will help."

Jazz turned from Mason to obey. Her hands were shaking as she opened her bag and laid out the stones, which winked in the dim light. Mason watched her a moment, his body stiff, unhappy, then he sank to his knees to help her. Jazz felt better with him near, his strong hands placing stones where she indicated.

"You'll have to leave," Zander was saying to Broderick. "Aleck reacts strongly to you, probably because you keep tranquing him. He knows you don't like him."

Broderick frowned and hefted the rifle. "I *like* him — at least when he's lucid. I just don't trust him."

"And that's why you have to go," Zander said. "Take the tranq gun too. It's making him nervous."

Mason looked up and gave his brother a nod. "It's all right, Brod. I got this. Zander's actually not as crazy as he seems."

Broderick didn't believe him, and Jazz knew Mason didn't really believe it either. But Mason was willing to do what it took to finish this.

Broderick considered for a time, then he slid the tranq rifle over his shoulder, dropped a key into Mason's hand, and made for the door. "I'll be right outside. Call me if you need another shot."

He gave Mason a long look then strode out and slammed the door behind him.

"Lock it," Zander said to Mason. "Just in case Aleck gets out. He'd make short work of that door, but at least it will slow him down so you and I can contain him. But if he makes it to the rest of the house ..."

Mason didn't like any part of what Zander said, Jazz could tell, but he climbed to his feet and locked the door.

Zander pointed at Jazz, his voice matter-of-fact despite the despair in his eyes. "*You*, sweetheart, pray to the Goddess as hard as you can. We'll need all the help she can give us. Mason, my friend, let me into the cage and then lock it behind me. Once Aleck is better, get him out of here but lock *me* in. Got it? You'll contain me in this good cage until I recover— if I can. If I can't ... " Zander paused, then he regarded them with resignation. "Kill me quickly and send for your Guardian."

Mason's face was drawn, but he nodded.

"Zander, don't," Jazz got to her feet and went to him. "I didn't realize he would be so bad. We can't ask you to do this." No wonder she and Mason had sensed fear in Zander—facing a crazed, strong beast who was too far insane to stop himself from killing, and maybe becoming just like him, was something no one should volunteer to do.

Zander looked down at her, his black eyes filled with acceptance. "You're sweet, Jazz. You and Mason make a great couple. But this is out of your hands now. I can't walk away from someone who needs my help any more than you can refuse to use your gift to search for someone because you're afraid of what you'll find. The Goddess picked me to do shit like this, so I'm gonna do it." He drew a long breath, took her hand, and squeezed it between his. "You and Mason concentrate on the stones and the Goddess, and put your strength together. I'll do my part, and ..." He shrugged. "We'll see what happens."

Zander needed to do this, Jazz suddenly understood. No matter how terrified he was of the feral, or of what the healing would do to him, Zander would go through with it. He had a drive to heal—he couldn't stop himself doing it any more than Jazz could stop psychic visions coming to her. He'd break into the cage regardless of whether Mason opened it for him.

Zander, without waiting for Mason's decision, began stripping off, ensuring he would be ready to shift.

Mason watched him a moment, then squared his shoulders with as much determination as Zander.

"Jasmine, go over there, and *stay* there until I get the cage locked again."

He pointed at the corner farthest from the cage door. Jazz, not really wanting to be in the path of a crazed feral Shifter, hurried to it.

Aleck caught her movement, turned his gaze to her, and kept it there. Jazz definitely didn't like that, but she lifted her chin and stared right back at him, keeping him distracted from Mason at the cage's door.

Broderick and his brothers had used a modified wrought-iron gate to secure the cage, its hinges welded into the bars. It had a deadbolt lock, which Mason opened with the key.

The moment the lock clicked open, Zander grabbed the gate, opened it, quickly slid through, and shut it behind him. Mason locked it immediately, leaving Zander alone in the cage with Aleck.

Aleck whipped his attention from Jazz to Zander. He stared at Zander in disbelief for a moment, then let out a roar and attacked him.

***

Mason clutched the bars, and Jasmine cried out as Aleck launched himself into Zander. The two Shifters met then became one ball of fighting madness.

Mason reached for the lock, but Zander bellowed at him, "*No!*" and shifted.

Aleck found himself caught in the strong arms of a man who was part human, part enormous polar bear. Zander snarled, going for Aleck with his teeth as Aleck clawed and fought. Neither Shifter wore a

Collar — there was nothing to stop them from tearing each other apart.

Jasmine hurried back to the cage. On her knees again, she continued to lay out her stones, chanting as she did so. Mason knelt beside her, following her directions to place the stones about two inches apart. She muttered over each one, though Mason could hear her words perfectly.

"Goddess, Mother of the Moon, attend us. Tiger's eye for protection; bloodstone for strength; amber, quartz, and amethyst for healing; obsidian for peace. We call you now to be with us."

Jasmine's invocation was not much different from what Shifters used for ceremonies or meditation. Mason began chanting along with her, figuring two people pleading for the Goddess's help would be better than one.

As they worked, Zander and Aleck fought. Zander was big, but Aleck was maddened by the crazy shit going on in his brain. There was no trace of the pain-in-the-ass Feline Nancy loved. Aleck was totally feral. His eyes were red, his mouth dripped froth, and he went for the kill without hesitation.

Jasmine lit her smudge stick, blowing on the embers to encourage the sage smoke to rise. A puff of it went past Mason, making him sneeze, and into the cage. Aleck coughed then tore himself from Zander, focused on Jasmine, and lunged straight at her.

Mason hauled Jasmine out of the way just as Aleck's clawed paws came through the bars, landing where Jasmine had knelt. The Goddess only knew what the claws of a feral would inject into human blood, if Jasmine had survived him ripping into her at all.

Zander took the opportunity to get behind Aleck and grab him in a headlock. Zander's white fur and burning black eyes made him look much like the yeti the hunters had feared him to be, a man-beast left over from primeval times. Zander had his huge hand-paws around Aleck's throat, and for a moment, Mason thought he'd snap Aleck's neck.

The moment passed. Zander dragged Aleck back from the bars and threw him to the floor. Zander went down on top of him, using his body weight to keep Aleck pinned. Aleck went crazy, flailing and crashing himself against the floor, trying to dislodge Zander.

Zander held him down with impossible strength, then to Mason's surprise, Zander closed his eyes and began to chant.

His voice rumbled through the basement room in a language Mason didn't recognize. The words were long and low, droned in a mesmerizing bass voice, a chant so ancient it vibrated Mason's bones. Mason didn't know how he knew the words were old, but his very cells recognized it must be so.

Aleck twisted and fought. Zander somehow held him in place, his chant continuing.

Jasmine seemed to understand what was needed. She lifted a piece of amethyst and clutched it tightly, then handed Mason the amber that had lit him up like a Christmas tree.

The amber wasn't glowing now, but Mason felt its warmth, palpable where it pressed his palm. Jasmine didn't wait for his reaction but grabbed his free hand.

A shock jolted from her body to his. Mason was filled with sudden heat, and not one that came from his ever-present need for her. Though his mating frenzy was never far from the surface, this was a connection, like a smooth cord forming around their joined hands and gathering into a knot.

The sage smoke filled Mason's nostrils, calming him in spite of the deathly struggle only four feet away.

At the same time, the amber in his hand began to glow. The yellow light leaked around Mason's fingers, surrounding his body and Jasmine's and then flowing from them into the cage.

Jasmine moved closer to him. Their hips and shoulders touched, and the amber's shine encompassed both of them. Jasmine glanced at Mason, as startled by all this as he was.

Mason looked down into Jasmine's wide blue eyes, and *knew.*

The amber glow touched Zander in the cage. He stiffened but chanted louder, his eerie words blending with the smoke and light.

Mason lost track of the world as Zander's voice transfixed him, as did the nearness of Jazz and her body pressed to his. A trembling warmth infused him, spreading out from his heart. It was pain but incredible joy at the same time, comparable to the exultation that had filled him when he'd thrust himself inside Jasmine for the first time and breathed his scent on her to make her his.

The mate bond.

Mason had no idea if Jasmine felt it too. Sometimes both halves of the couple didn't manifest it. Heartbreaking and devastating when that didn't happen.

Figured that Mason would have to realize it *here*, where an insane polar bear and a feral Feline were battling it out while magic Mason didn't believe in swirled around him. That magic, the metaphysical world Jasmine had introduced him to, was now the only thing that might save their butts.

He felt Jasmine looking at him with encouragement. She was, in the middle of all this, trying to make *Mason* feel better. That's what true mates did — looked out for each other, protected each other, loved each other, healed each other. *The touch of a mate.*

If they survived this, their lovemaking was going to blow off the roof.

Mason glanced at Aleck again and blinked. Had he calmed? It wasn't obvious if so, but Mason swore Aleck's writhing had grown less frenzied, and he was now only trying to disembowel Zander a few times a minute.

A sort of fog began to permeate the cage, but not from the smoke. Mason, blinking, realized the fog wasn't really there, only something he was seeing with his mind's eye.

Auras, he understood with a shock. Mason was seeing what Jasmine saw — the manifestation of what made a person who he or she was.

Zander's was gray and black in various shades, while Aleck's was black streaked with violent red. Jasmine, by his side, was silver and a beautiful, tranquil blue, shot here and there with rainbow colors. Exactly right for her.

As Mason turned back to the cage, his hold on Jasmine's hand tightening, he noted that the red in Aleck's aura was gradually fading.

Whatever the hell Zander was doing was working. Mason saw the amber glow from the stone that enveloped Mason and Jasmine now sliding into Zander's and Aleck's auras.

He and Jasmine were somehow causing that, he realized. However the Goddess-touched part of Mason was twining with the Goddess in Jasmine, it was coming together to lend Zander and Aleck strength.

Under Zander, Aleck drew a shuddering breath. He slowly ceased struggling and then simply lay still, pinned by Zander and breathing hard.

After a few more minutes, Aleck shifted haltingly back to his human form and tried to lift his head. He saw Mason and looked at him, his eyes normal green and no longer tinged red. "Oh, Goddess," Aleck said in a weak voice as Zander slid away from him. "What have I done now?"

Mason got to his knees, the amber light fading. "Easy," Mason said. "You all right?"

Aleck's head thumped down to the cement floor. "Did I hurt Nancy? Please, please say I didn't—"

"Nancy is fine," Jasmine said quickly. "So's the cub she's carrying. I think he's okay now, Zander." She came to Mason, resting her hand on his shoulder as she peered into the cage at Zander. "Are *you* all right?"

Zander, whose back had been turned, suddenly faced them. He had shifted all the way to polar bear, and the black in his eyes was like windows to nothing. At the same time, the last of the violent streaks in Aleck's aura drained completely away and dove into Zander's.

Zander rose to huge bear feet, his snarls hard, vicious, and bloodthirsty. The feral rage that had been inside Aleck was rising anew in a polar bear who could wipe out every person in this house, and probably this Shiftertown.

Mason was up even before Jasmine shouted at him to get Broderick and the tranq gun. Mason never had the chance. Zander slammed himself into the gate full force, and it bent on its hinges. Mason threw himself between the cage and Jasmine, just before the gate broke fully and a ton of polar bear landed on him. He heard Jasmine screaming for Broderick as she unlocked and wrenched open the door.

Aleck remained huddled in the cage, dumbfounded. Zander slammed Mason to the floor with one giant paw full of razor-sharp claws, all trace of sanity gone.

Mason didn't dare shift, knowing he'd be nearly helpless in the moments between forms. In those moments, Zander could kill him. He staved off the bear the best he could and heard Broderick stomping in, swearing a blue streak as only Broderick could.

Then came the thunk of the tranquilizer gun and Zander's roar as the dart went into him.

Zander yanked himself away from Mason, but he didn't look in the least subdued. He roared as he rose higher and higher on his back legs, and Broderick said, "Well, fuck."

Mason rolled out from under Zander, shifting as he went, his clothes ripping away. Zander landed on all fours and shook himself, sending the tranq dart flying.

Zander barreled toward Broderick and Jasmine, who were in front of the door. Mason landed on Zander's back, but the bear easily threw him off. Broderick was able to yank Jasmine out of the way as Zander slammed past them, tearing through the door and doorframe, and headed up the stairs.

Mason, fully wolf now, sprinted after him.

Chapter Fifteen

Mason was right on Zander's heels as they reached the ground floor of the house. He grabbed at Zander's back legs, terrified the bear would dash to the second floor and tear through the rest of his family, but Zander crashed out the kitchen door and into the sunshine.

Great. Instead of a polar bear wreaking havoc in Mason's house, he was going to wreak it in the rest of Shiftertown.

Zander was *fast.* He took off down the street, muscles rippling under his fur as he ran. Other Shifters out and about were sensible enough to get the hell out of the way, even as they gaped at seeing a polar bear charge down the street. Polar bears were very rare, and a full-grown one had never been seen in this Shiftertown. News of him would run from one side of town to the other in about five minutes.

Mason couldn't take the time to shift back to human, but he glared at the Lupines he passed, willing them to understand him.

Find Tiger. Get Tiger. Would you go?

Zander fortunately didn't stop to attack any of the other Shifters, though he roared at them if they came too close. He was making a solid line for something — Mason had no idea what.

Wolves were fast too. Mason ran like hell, his paws pounding on the street or in dirt where Zander detoured through yards. Mason plowed up flowerbeds and scattered cubs' toys. He'd hear about it later, but right now, he had to stop a crazed bear.

As the houses flowed past, Mason finally realized where Zander was headed. One house sat back from the street among tall trees, the two-story bungalow reinforced for the strength of those who lived in it. They'd enclosed the garage and now called it the Den, in the humorous way of bears.

Zander was heading for Ronan's house. Ronan was a Kodiak bear, as was his roommate and member of his clan, Rebecca. Both were mated now to humans and the house was full of cubs, most of them adopted, orphaned bears no one else had been able to take care of. The oldest had just passed his Transition from cub to adulthood, but the others — Cherie, Olaf, and small Katie, plus Ronan's tiny cub — were too young to defend themselves.

Mason put on a burst of speed. He managed to get around Zander — leaping over a hedge to do so — and landed in front of the house's back porch, whirling around and bracing himself to face Zander.

Zander was completely feral. Any semblance of the sort-of crazy, kind-of affable bear-man in his

messy trailer in Alaska was gone. In its place was a
monster of a polar bear, savage and enraged. He'd
not wanted to come down here and try to heal a
feral, for crap's sake, but he'd done it, and now he
was paying the price.

So was Mason. Zander attacked him.

As Mason went down under the huge black
claws, he heard the other bears come out. Ronan's
ferocious roar shook the yard, Rebecca's not much
less powerful one behind him. The door of the Den
banged open, and Mason heard human footsteps—
that would be Walker, Rebecca's mate, a military guy
who would have all kinds of weapons.

Zander fought wildly. He smacked Mason aside,
Mason tumbling until he slammed up against the
side of the porch, pain searing his ribs. Ronan, nearly
as enormous as Zander, barreled at him, but Zander,
far gone in insanity, shoved him aside as though he
weighed nothing.

Ronan and Rebecca went after Zander again, both
bears now, but their Collars sparked hard, slowing
them down and zapping the strength they needed.
Zander was going to get around them into the house
where Ronan's mate and the vulnerable cubs were.

Walker had a tranq rifle, but he was trying to find
a decent shot, not wanting to hit the others by
mistake. Even a tranq might not do any good.
Zander had brushed off the one Broderick had fired
right into him. Broderick hadn't missed—Zander
had just not noticed the tranq.

Zander fought hard with Rebecca and then Ronan
again, before he swiped them both aside, Rebecca's
fur bloody, sprinted up to the porch, and hit the
house's back door.

Mason was on him. Snarling, his Collar throwing sparks deep into both his and Zander's fur, Mason got his teeth around Zander's neck and hung on. He willed Walker to grab a real gun and shoot, but if Walker hit Mason, that wouldn't help. Mason couldn't risk jumping off Zander to give Walker a better shot, because in that moment, Zander would get into the house.

Zander bucked and shook, trying to dislodge Mason. They both crashed against the porch's railing, which splintered and broke, sending the two of them down into the yard.

Mason kept hold of Zander, determined he wouldn't make it up to the porch again. Where the hell was Tiger? He was the only one big enough and tough enough to take down a feral polar bear. Tiger didn't wear a real Collar, so he had nothing to get in his way.

But if Tiger was off doing something or other for Dylan, it might be a long time before he was tracked down and able to get back. Meanwhile, Zander could do a lot of damage.

As Mason tried desperately to get his teeth into Zander's throat, he heard Broderick and Jasmine running into the yard, Broderick demanding that the bears get off their asses and help Mason. *They're trying, bro.* Broderick was always so impatient.

He also heard Jasmine scream.

The sound went right through him, galvanizing Mason with new energy. He had no idea why Jasmine screamed—Zander was busy pulverizing Mason, so she hadn't been hurt.

But his mate was in distress, and Mason's instinct was to protect her, no matter who he had to kill to do it. His Collar increased its sparks, but Mason barely felt them as he sank his teeth into Zander's neck.

Rebecca's roars and then Ronan's rose, both of them panicking, and Walker yelled, "No! Stop him!"

Zander gave one final shake that dislodged Mason. Mason's mouth was ripped away from Zander's fur, Mason crashing hard to the ground. He heard something snap, and then pain so intense burst through him that his vision went dark.

Through the blur Mason saw what everyone had been yelling about.

A very small white bear with soot-black eyes had appeared on the porch. It stood on the edge, where the railing had broken, and stared in amazement at Zander.

Rebecca, human now, was trying to reach him, and waving at the young woman inside the back door — another of the cubs — to stay there.

Zander ran right at the polar bear cub — and stopped.

Olaf stared down at Zander with no fear. He let out a little growl, one that held both curiosity and warning. *This is my territory. Who are* you?

Mason tried to leap up and put himself between them, but his leg was broken, and he fell back down with a yelp. The others, he noted, weren't moving either, only stared at Olaf and Zander, frozen in place.

Jasmine broke away from Broderick, darted to Mason, and fell to her knees beside him, her hands going to his fur. Under her touch, Mason's pain eased the slightest bit.

Zander had gone utterly still. His eyes were red, no sanity in them, but he gazed at Olaf in silence.

Olaf, curiosity overcoming caution, hurtled himself off the porch, landed on clumsy feet, and closed the short distance between himself and the bigger polar bear.

Ronan did move then, the Kodiak heading straight for Olaf, but Zander turned on him and let out a roar. Zander positioned himself between Ronan and Olaf. Not to hurt Olaf, Mason realized after one foggy moment, but to protect him.

Olaf batted Zander's back leg. Zander turned around, very slowly, and lowered his head toward Olaf's. Olaf put both paws on Zander's face and drew himself up to look right into Zander's eyes.

The red in them started to fade. Zander took a long breath, and then another as Olaf peered at him, trying to figure out who was this gigantic bear that looked like him.

Zander lifted a great paw and placed it, very gently, on Olaf's back. Olaf growled in delight and rolled out from under Zander's touch, dancing up, his body wriggling.

Zander lowered himself down, groaning as though the movement hurt him, settling on his belly. Olaf licked the top of Zander's nose, then scampered up over Zander's huge head to his back.

Jasmine drew a sharp breath as Olaf scrambled past the muzzle that had been so ferociously biting everything in sight, but Zander did nothing. Olaf happily bounced on Zander's back, and Zander rolled over with another groan.

Zander ended up on his back, his feet splaying, grunting as Olaf landed on his stomach. The bears and Mason, Broderick and Walker tensed, but Zander let out another long breath and eased himself into the grass. Olaf perched happily on Zander's chest, letting out little huffs of breath. The feral beast in Zander dissipated and flowed away.

Jasmine leaned down and kissed Mason between his wolf ears. "Now, isn't that the cutest thing you ever saw?"

Mason made a wolf noise in return. He was in pain, but Jasmine near him was a fine thing.

He heard more footsteps approaching, hard and fast. Tiger came charging into the yard, followed by Dylan, Tiger with a tranq rifle. Tiger halted when he saw the large polar bear lying limply on his back, the smaller bear contentedly on top of him.

"Looks like we won't need this," Tiger said in his rumbling voice as he upended the rifle.

He glanced over at Mason and Jasmine and gave Mason an approving nod. *Well done,* he seemed to say, but Tiger, never eloquent, only turned his head to watch Zander and Olaf again, unconcerned.

If Tiger thought all was well, Mason knew, then it was. He laid his head on Jasmine's lap, liking how she stroked a gentle hand through his fur, and proceeded to pass out.

***

Mason's leg was shattered. Jazz watched worriedly as the Kodiak bears and Walker loaded Mason into the back of Dylan's pickup. Walker, a medic, had quickly splinted Mason's leg when he was human again—Mason hadn't been able to stop the shift. Mason had insisted on being taken home instead of a hospital or even into the bears' house.

"Just make sure that damned polar bear saves Aunt Cora," Mason told Jazz between his teeth as Dylan drove them down the block.

Zander returned to Mason's house on foot, still bear, Olaf as cub riding on his back. Zander walked into the yard at the same time the pickup reached the house. Broderick himself lifted Mason from the bed of the truck and carried him into the living room.

"Upstairs," Mason snapped when Broderick wanted to lay him on the sofa. "My room."

"Hey, I'm not your litter bearer," Broderick growled, but he carried his youngest brother upstairs with a gentleness Jazz suspected he'd used with Mason all his life.

Mason's bedroom looked as though a tornado had blown through it, and his bed had been broken. Someone had leaned the wooden head and footboards against the wall but the mattress lay alone on the floor. Broderick set Mason carefully on the mattress, Mason grunting as his leg settled.

Jazz wanted to stay with Mason, but he waved her off. "No—make sure Aunt Cora's all right. I trust you. *Please.*"

His worry was greater than his pain, Jazz saw. She kissed him gently, gave him an amethyst to hold, and hurried into the hall.

Zander was coming up the stairs, his clothing resumed, minus the duster. He gave Jazz a long look, his eyes haunted. Behind him scampered the polar bear cub, as though he didn't want to let Zander out of his sight. Zander reached down and picked up Olaf, carrying him in his arms into Aunt Cora's room.

Nancy and Joanne weren't there—they were downstairs helping Aleck. Aunt Cora didn't even open her eyes when Jazz and Zander came in, too weak to respond. Her aura was dark, sticky, fading.

208 Jennifer Ashley

Zander set Olaf on the sofa, knelt by Aunt Cora's bed, and took her hand in his.

Zander healed her. While Jazz sat with her arms around the cub, Olaf watching with big black eyes, Zander went into his chanting ritual. Derek and Corey, who'd come upstairs to keep an eye on Zander, didn't look impressed, but they only watched.

A few minutes into Zander's chant, Aunt Cora began to breathe easier, her chest rising and falling without labor. Another ten minutes after this, she opened her eyes, gazed at Zander's bowed head and long white braids, and said, "What are you doing back here?"

"Healing you, ma'am," Zander mumbled.

Jazz saw the thick streaks of pain and fever that had threaded Aunt Cora's aura flow into Zander's, staining it black. Maybe that was why Zander's aura was so neutral, Jazz pondered. He easily absorbed whatever tainted his patients.

As the viscid murk of Aunt Cora's suffering left her, Zander let out a pained breath, lost hold of her hands, and collapsed to the floor.

Olaf bounded down from the sofa and went to him, making distressed little noises. Jazz took an extra blanket that had been folded on a chair and gently draped it over him. She smoothed his hair from his hot forehead as Olaf lay down right next to him, snuggling his furry body into Zander's shoulder. Zander only groaned again, his eyes fluttering as though unaware of what they did.

"Well," Aunt Cora said, voice weak. She looked at Zander on the floor and Olaf pressed against him. "What do you know about that? Help me up,

Jasmine, sweetheart. We need to find someplace soft for him to sleep."

***

"Ow!" Mason yelled.

"Don't be a baby," Zander snapped, his hands on Mason's broken leg. "Your auntie was hurt worse than you, and she didn't say a word."

Pain suffused Mason's body, obscuring the world. The only clear spot in his life was Jasmine, her hand in his.

Mason growled. "That's because Aunt Cora didn't have a fucking huge polar bear pressing down on her broken leg."

"You want it to heal?" Zander said without heat. "Stop moving."

"Look at me, Mason." Jasmine's voice cut through the anguish. "Just look at me."

She touched his face, turning his head on the pillow. Jasmine sat beside him, her hip against his, her cool fingers wrapped around his hot ones.

Mason liked looking at her. "You're beautiful," he said.

Jasmine's blue eyes warmed, and her nose wrinkled with her smile. "You're not so bad yourself."

"Yeah? I thought you didn't like Shifters."

Jasmine shrugged. "I'll make an exception." She kissed Mason's fist. "You're pretty exceptional."

"Can I make an observation?" Zander raised his head, the ends of his braids brushing Mason's leg.

"No," Mason said, at the same time Jasmine said, "Yes."

Zander chuckled in spite of the pain in his eyes. He'd barely recovered from curing Aunt Cora, and now he was in here trying to help Mason. The man's courage was remarkable, and Mason warmed with gratitude to him.

"You two kids belong together," Zander said. "Make the mate-claim, Mason. I'll witness it."

Jasmine looked startled. "Mate-claim?" Her voice turned cautious. "What does that mean, exactly?"

Zander answered before Mason could. "Means he's making it clear he wants to take you as mate, under the sun and moon ceremonies that Shifters recognize as official. Means no other Shifter can claim you without fighting him for it. Kind of like an engagement, but with more sex and violence."

Jasmine looked at Mason again, her expression holding trepidation. "Mason, I ..."

"You don't have to accept," Mason said quickly, a heavy lump burning in his chest. "You can go back home to your life and your crazy house. I live in Shiftertown with too many brothers and assorted relatives. I make guitars and music boxes in a hidden shop. Although if I'm mated, Derek and Corey might stop giving me so much shit. You could be my protector."

Mason heard the cynicism in his voice but he couldn't stop it. He could offer Jasmine nothing but himself, and he knew it. Sure, his family had as much stashed away as any Shifters did, but he didn't want a woman to accept him for his family's hoard. Mason wanted Jasmine to like him for himself, no matter how much of a wreck he was.

"Hmm, that sounded like a mate-claim to me," Zander said. "I'm witness."

Jasmine leaned down to Mason and looked right into his eyes. "You get better. We'll talk later, when you're not in so much pain."

The pain was already better. Zander's hands on his leg no longer hurt.

"Yeah," he said to Jasmine and inhaled the fragrance of her hair. "We'll talk later."

Zander's face paled, his cheekbones standing out in his graying face. He gave a sudden sharp cry and let go of Mason to fall to the floor, clutching his own leg in agony.

Jasmine left the bed, snatched up a quilt from the bottom of it, and draped it kindly over Zander. "Can I get you anything?" she leaned down to ask him.

Silently, Zander shook his head. Mason understood, from what Jasmine had told him after Zander had healed Aunt Cora, that the pain he took on simply had to run its course.

The door opened and Olaf, a white-haired little boy once more, dressed in T-shirt and jeans, came briskly in. He carried a small pillow which he arranged beneath Zander's head. Olaf then sat down next to Zander and looked up at Jasmine.

"It's all right," he said with the wisdom of his ten years. "He's a polar bear, like me. I'll take care of him, now."

Chapter Sixteen

Zander Moncrieff met Dylan Morrissey a few days later at the house of the bears.

Because polar bears were rare in the Shifter world, Zander wondered if Olaf and he were of the same clan. Mason had told him Olaf's parents had been shot, which pissed off Zander to no end. It was pathetic that shit like that happened when you were a Shifter.

Zander had considered taking Olaf back up north with him, but he'd realized in the time he'd been in this Shiftertown that the little guy was very happy living with his surrogate parents and the other cubs. Zander sought an isolated existence to protect himself, but that would be no life for a parentless cub. All those who lived in the bears' house loved Olaf, Zander could see, and so here he would stay.

Dylan Morrissey was a different matter altogether. Dylan was Feline, and Zander didn't get along much with Felines. Wolves yes — he felt some affinity with wolves. Cats drove him crazy.

Dylan was a venerable Shifter, about at his third century. He was by no means a spent force, however. Despite the gray at his temples, he was as vigorous as his sons, and he had the weight of experience and wisdom behind him. Liam Morrissey might run the Austin Shiftertown, but Dylan ran everything else.

"Amazing what you did," Dylan said as the two of them stood alone in the yard between the bears' back porch and the Den. "Ferals that far gone usually can't be helped."

Zander shrugged, trying to push aside the dark horror that had taken over his brain when Aleck's insanity had infused him. He hadn't remembered who he was, where he was, not even his own name, even though his mother had pounded the three names into him from childhood. Only the shock of seeing the polar bear cub, the knowledge that he had to protect the little guy from all danger, including himself, had stopped him. The feral-like state he'd experienced hadn't been true like Aleck's — Zander took on only the *feeling* of what he healed, not the actual malady — but it had been bloody close enough. He'd feared something even worse — that he'd not be able to come out of it and would die like that. One day, he might have to go too far to heal someone and never recover — it was a real possibility.

"What can I say?" Zander said, trying to keep his voice light. "It's a gift."

"It is," Dylan agreed mildly. "One I can use."

Zander's blood went cold. "No, no, no." He shook his head, kept on shaking it. "I don't have my phone number listed for a reason. If I don't spend a certain amount of time alone, I can't do what I do. Pen me up, stick me in a Shiftertown, and I'm no good to anyone."

"You misunderstand," Dylan said. "Live where you want, take as much alone time as you need. You don't have a Collar; you can live among humans if you're careful. But be around when I need you."

Zander gave him a flat look. "I'm not in your clan, Morrissey. Not even in your jurisdiction."

Dylan made an indifferent gesture, an economic movement he'd no doubt perfected over many decades. "There are things going on here in South Texas, Shifter things, that I don't like. You're a strong fighter, and a good healer. At least stay for a while and help me out."

Zander held up his hands. "Nice of you to ask, Dylan, but what I really need is time to wander the wilderness."

Dylan's gaze sharpened. "I'm not asking, lad." His eyes were blue, and the force of his stare showed how alpha he truly was. Even Zander had a hard time meeting those eyes. "You endangered my people. The outcome was good, but you should have warned them better, taken precautions. You stopped in time, but it could have been so much worse."

Zander knew that. He'd seriously injured Mason, a young man he wanted to call friend, and he could have killed even the Kodiak bears and all their cubs. He'd been a monster, and it would take him a long time to forget the nightmare of that.

Zander blew out a breath, stuffed his hands into his duster's pockets, and looked around. "You know, Austin's a pretty cool place. I might stick around a while. Take in the sights, check out the music scene, find an apartment near good eats ..."

Dylan gave him a nod. "Keep your cell phone on. I'll introduce you to another un-Collared Shifter I'm having help me. Name of Kendrick."

He watched Zander expectantly, but Zander drew a blank. "Never heard of him."

"Hmm," Dylan said shortly. "You will."

And the conversation was done.

Zander spent some time visiting with Olaf, going bear for him so the two could romp in the yard. Then he returned to the McNaughton house, planning to gather his things and ask the human ladies there if they could steer him in the direction of a place to live.

Dylan was right—because Zander didn't have a Collar, no one needed to know he was Shifter. He'd move in among humans and blend in, like he always did.

Okay, so he wasn't always all that blendy, but he'd learned how to make humans accept him and not betray him.

The first two people he saw when he walked up to the house were Aleck, no longer feral, and his very pregnant mate, Nancy. Nancy was planted on top of Aleck's lap, they were nuzzling, and looked very, very happy.

They both rose as Zander approached. Aleck wore a clean shirt and jeans, his dark hair was combed, and he gave Zander an affable smile. He looked exhausted, but sane and much relieved.

"Thank you," Aleck said when Zander reached the porch. Zander remained on the top step, leaning on the railing and watching the lovebirds. "I can't believe you did something like that for me," Aleck went on. "For my mate and cub." He drew Nancy closer. The lines of strain around her eyes had gone, and her mouth had softened.

"Hey, I like a happy ending," Zander said. "But don't waste thanks on me. Thank Mason and Jazz. They worked their asses off trying to find me, went through a lot. They deserve a truckload of praise."

Aleck flushed but nodded. "I know. I've been a shit to Mason." He drew Nancy closer and kissed her temple. "Don't worry. I'll make it up to both of them."

"When they get back from New Orleans," Nancy went on, her look knowing. Mason had left early this morning to take Jazz back there. Their good-byes to Zander had been cursory, both Mason and Jazz tense. "They need some time alone to figure it all out."

Zander's heart lightened. "I think they'll make it. And then I'll take credit for bringing them together." He pointed both forefingers at Nancy and Aleck. "You two kids take care of yourselves."

He swept past them into the house, asked his questions of Joanne and the brothers, grabbed his stuff, and left Shiftertown.

***

Jazz stood on the steps of her grandmother's front porch and watched Mason dismount his motorcycle. They hadn't spoken much as they'd made the long ride from Austin to New Orleans.

Jazz hadn't seen a lot of Mason in the days before they'd left Austin. She'd been busy helping the ladies in Broderick's household get things back together, and Mason had absented himself from the house most of the time.

While Aunt Cora had been healed, she'd been weak but too stubborn to admit it. Jazz hadn't wanted to leave Joanne to run the house by herself. Aleck had been weak as well, and Nancy spent all her time doting on him until Mason's brothers claimed they would pass out from all the sweetness in the house.

As a result, Jazz had seen almost nothing of Mason once he could get out of bed again. He'd been working on her guitar, she knew, but he said very little to her when he did come home.

He only made love to her in the silence of the night, rocking into her in hard, desperate strokes, then kissing her until they both wound down into sleep. Talking had been pushed aside, both of them knowing that the wrong word at the wrong time could shatter the bubble they'd formed around themselves.

Now Jazz watched Mason approach the house, as she had days and days ago, and was again blown away by his physical strength and his aura.

Mason unstrapped the repaired guitar from where it had ridden in its case and carried it up the walk. He hesitated at the bottom step of the porch, looking at the spread of the house, the veranda, the gingerbread trim, the flowering vines.

"Sure the cops are done with this place?" he asked.

Late afternoon light dappled Mason's dark hair and touched his light gray eyes as he assessed the house, looking for danger. The only reason Jazz had walked up here and unlocked the door was that she'd not listened to Mason when he'd growled at her to wait. Besides, she had the key.

"Pretty sure," Jazz said. "I told my friend at Inspirations to tell the cops that Lucas broke in and started shooting up the place, and I hightailed it out of town. Then he trapped himself under the stairs. Lucas apparently was babbling something about wolves and ghosts when they rescued him, and he was taken away, suspected of being high or crazy."

Mason didn't smile. He completed his once-over of the house and mounted the steps. He brushed past Jazz, his nearness making her burn, and walked inside.

He stood in the hall and inhaled, taking in the scents, testing the air, before he nodded and motioned Jazz to come in.

"You don't have to do that," Jazz said as she dropped her bag in the hall. "I can sense auras. I know no one's here and that the house is glad to see us."

Mason gave her a long look. "It doesn't matter. I'll always protect you."

Jazz's blood heated at the dark note in his voice. So few men she'd dated had even noticed she was in the room with them unless they wanted sex. The exception had been the Feline Shifter, and she'd mistaken his focus for love.

Mason turned and walked into the dining room, the double pocket doors standing open. The long dining table, a relic of the eighteenth century, stood waiting for meals that hadn't been set on it in years.

Mason put the table to a different purpose now. He opened the soft-lined case he'd found for the guitar, lifted the repaired instrument from it, and laid it on the table.

Sunlight filtered through the vine-shrouded windows to touch the polished wood, and Jazz's eyes widened in awe. Mason had cut a new front and back for the guitar, but instead of leaving it plain as the old guitar had been, he'd used an exotic wood, a warm golden red with wide stripes, and embellished it with inlay.

"Koa," Mason said, touching the guitar with blunt fingers. "Ukuleles are made out of it. It's got a rich, mellow sound, especially on an acoustic guitar."

Inlay made of a tiny band of crushed stones ran along the rim between the guitar's top and body, and around the rosette that bordered the hole in the center. The work was so fine that a lump formed in Jazz's throat.

"Mason, it's beautiful." Her eyes stung with tears as she looked up at him. "No wonder I didn't see you for days."

Mason cleared his throat, cheekbones flushing. "I wanted to get it just right. It needs to cure for a while, so be careful with it."

"Can I play it?" The sudden urge to hold the guitar, to hear it, welled up inside Jazz and wouldn't leave her alone.

Mason considered. "Sure. Wouldn't hurt for now."

He lifted the guitar but instead of handing the instrument to her, he carried it out of the room and down the hall to the veranda.

Jazz followed him to the shady gazebo, which would be a special place to Jazz from now on, where she and Mason had shared their first kiss. She warmed at the memory, wanting to laugh at the clumsy way she'd launched herself at him.

Mason handed Jazz the guitar while he put the table and chairs to rights and cleaned up what Lucas had knocked over. Then he sat down in the chair next to hers, took the guitar again, and tuned it for her.

He did it quickly, bending his head to listen as he tightened and loosened strings, needing no gadget to tell him when the note was true. Some people could tune instruments by ear—apparently Mason was one of them.

Mason gave Jazz back the guitar, then leaned his elbows on his knees and made a quick gesture with his fingers. "Go ahead."

Self-consciously, Jazz placed her fingers on the fretboard, her right hand ready to strum. The guitar felt good, the strings hovering close to the refitted neck but not too tight, the familiarity of the guitar's curve on her leg comforting.

Jazz knew she didn't play very well—she simply loved to play. There was no concert hall in her future, and that was fine with her. Some things should be done for the pure enjoyment of them.

She fingered an E chord and strummed her right hand over the strings. A sweet, mellow sound came forth, which was partly the voice of the old Martin, partly the richness Mason had instilled in it. She switched to an A minor, with its darker tone, hearing an entirely different facet to the guitar.

Jazz drew a breath. "Mason, this is—"

Mason fixed her with a gray gaze. "Just play."

Jazz closed her mouth, strummed a few more chords, and then began the song her grandmother liked, the one she'd sung for Mason when he'd first asked her to play.

She fumbled with the changes as she always did, her voice cracking with emotion. She pictured her grandmother in the background, nodding her encouragement. Then her grandmother faded, and it was just Mason, watching her with those moon-gray eyes.

Jazz faltered to a halt. Mason reached out and touched her cheek.

"Stay with me," he said. His words were soft, blending with the whisper of wind in the roses.

Jazz tried a smile, her heart beating hard. "This is my house."

"You know what I mean." Mason didn't look away from her, his touch strengthening, his voice clear. "I made a mate-claim. You never answered."

Pain stabbed at her. Jazz slid the guitar from her lap, carefully setting it in the stand that was its home. "Because I know about Shifters. I love you, Mason, but I can't face the day when you come to me and tell me you formed this mate bond with another Shifter and have to leave. That would kill me. Please, don't make me go through that. Better to have a clean break right now, right?"

Tears filled her voice. Mason's brows came down as his face darkened with fury.

"The Feline you went out with was a fuck-wad," he said in a hard voice. "He should have told you he hadn't formed the mate bond with you, and that he could form it with someone else." Mason put his fist on his chest, over his heart. "*I* don't have that problem. The mate bond grabbed me, and I know it. It reached out and snared me when you sat here and kissed me in this very spot, and it hasn't let me go since. Maybe you didn't form it for me; I don't know. Doesn't matter. You're my mate. Always will be, even if you run off with some other dickhead like Lucas or that dumb-ass Feline."

Jazz's lips parted, her fingers going numb. "What are you talking about?"

"I'm talking about *me* forming the mate bond for you," Mason said steadily. "It means I'll always be bound to you, no matter what. I'll protect you and love you. Forever. You're my *mate*." Mason tapped his chest as he spoke then he returned his hands to his knees. "You read auras. *Look*."

Jazz forced herself to calm. She unclouded her thoughts, let the warm breeze blow the scent of roses to her, and studied the man she loved with her inner mind's eye.

Mason's aura was as hot and strong as ever — gray shot with golden streaks the color of the amber. But something had changed from the first time she'd looked at it. Mason's aura surrounded him like a cloud of mist, and in the center of it, right over his heart, fire blossomed. It was a deeper gold in the midst of his golden hue, its center red hot.

Under Jazz's scrutiny, the fire grew brighter, tendrils of it reaching from Mason to Jazz. She jumped as the stream of this fire touched and met the glow that burned in the center of Jazz herself.

That fire now pounded through her heart. Jazz found herself smiling hard, her mouth almost aching as she felt something inside her complete, the acknowledgment that she'd found the other half of her whole.

She stretched out her hand and touched his face.

"I love you, Mason." Jazz laughed, the laughter filling her with effervescent happiness. "What the hell have you done to me?"

The heat in Mason's eyes flared. "I haven't done a damned thing. A mate bond has a mind of its own. We're helpless in its power." He said the words with an ironic twist, then flattened his mouth in the next moment. "That means—I love you back, Jasmine. My mate. Stay with me."

Jazz lifted one of his hands, touching the hard, work-worn fingers that had wrought such beauty into her beloved guitar. Her heart was full, all that was lonely dissolving into a breath and flying away on the warm May breeze.

"I'm not going anywhere," she said softly.

Mason's face changed. He went from a wolf silently waiting to see what she would do to a man who had been suddenly plunged into fierce elation. He reached out and hauled Jazz onto his lap so quickly she had no opportunity to do anything ungraceful like lose her balance and fall.

She rested on his strong thigh, his arms around her. The porch floor creaked, a tiny rumble running through it.

The vibration increased as Mason kissed her, his mouth opening hers, his tongue hot and strong. The vines rattled and the wind chimes began dancing.

Jazz eased back, Mason kissing the corner of her lips. "I think the house likes us doing this," she said.

Mason's eyes had darkened to smoke gray. "Good."

He lifted her into his arms and carried her across the veranda and into the house. Mason swarmed up the stairs that had so readily swallowed Lucas and unerringly found Jazz's bedroom. He set her on the rumpled sheets and leaned over her.

"I hope the house likes this too," he said, his voice a rumble. He skimmed Jazz's top from her, loosening the bra she'd bought in Austin. He made impatient noises as he worked, and she caught mutters about why females insisted on confining themselves.

Jazz had her hands on his waistband, busily opening his jeans. "I could ask the same thing," she said. "So many layers, when you look just fine without them."

Mason stepped back and shoved off his clothes with his usual quickness. Jazz had already learned to let him, to sit back and enjoy watching his tight body come into view. Mason tossed away his T-shirt, his lower body already bare. His cock was tight and lifting toward her, beckoning her hands.

Jazz caught it, liking how Mason didn't mind her tugging him to her with it. He came down to the bed without hesitation, sunlight kissing his skin as he drew off Jazz's jeans and underwear.

They landed together in the bed where Jazz had dreamed so many dreams. Mason kissed her lips, her face, her throat.

A noise like a sigh went through the house as Mason slid inside her, drowned by Jazz's cry of delight. She pulled him into her, hands on his back, his firm hips, as he began to thrust.

"My mate," Mason said, voice going wolf-like. The last of the sun's rays hugged them, the warm air dampening their skin. Mason traced her cheek, his eyes gray and intense. "I love you, Jasmine. Mate of my heart."

"Love you too," was all Jazz could say before wildness took her, and she was crying out.

The house rattled, but maybe it was only the bed banging the wall as Mason drove into her until they both were crazed with it.

***

Mason didn't sleep afterward. He was too keyed up, the mate bond pounding through him, too *happy* for the first time in his life. His loneliness, his disconnectedness from his brothers, was gone. He had Jasmine, who was beautiful inside and out, watching him with her blue eyes.

Mason lay propped on his side next to her, both of them on top of the covers. This way, he could study her body in the dusk, lean down and kiss her skin, trace the flower under her nipple with his tongue.

He would buy her a sarong, one that would hug her body and let almost all of the tattoo show. A sarong would be easily stripped away any time mating frenzy hit them. Mason figured it would be hitting him again and again for a very long time.

Jasmine gave him a languid smile and tucked one hand behind her head. The movement stretched her body enticingly.

"So how do we make this work?" she asked him. "You talk about living in a filled house like it's a bad thing. I love family—I like *your* family. I think what you have is wonderful."

"You might not after you've lived there a while." Mason traced the vine all the way around her breast. "After Broderick has rampaged through the house, and my brothers snarl, my aunt yells at everyone, and Shifters and their mates have loud and endless sex."

Jasmine only laughed. "Sounds great."

"There's always the safe house," Mason said. "It's quiet there."

"Sure," Jasmine answered, looking content. "A fine place to get away from it all. I like that house too."

"And this one." Mason looked up at the beamed ceiling, the boards between the beams slightly bowed, like a smile. "We can come here as often as you want. As long as I don't get caught trying to travel outside my state."

Jasmine's grin beamed out, her blue eyes like a warm evening sky. "I'll protect you," she said. "The house will too."

"Great," Mason said, pretending dismay. "I've gotta trust my safety to a building that swallows people."

"It won't eat you," Jasmine promised. "It likes you."

"It must." Mason smoothed back her hair, his fingers lingering in the natural brown that showed more each day. "It's letting me stay here and love you."

Jasmine reached for him, drawing him down to her warmth and softness. "Speaking of that ..."

Mason pulled her close and slid into her, kissing her as he went. He began to love her again, slowly this time, the two of them wrapping around each other as the fire of the mate bond flowed through them and made them one.

A breeze sighed through the house, and Mason swore he heard it chuckle in satisfaction.

Out in the gazebo, the same wind stirred the strings of the guitar, its breath joining the louder music of the wind chimes before floating into the sultriness of the warm spring night.

End

Please continue for a preview of

White Tiger

Book 8
of the

Shifters Unbound series

by

Jennifer Ashley

White Tiger

Chapter One

It was almost time. Addison Price slid the coffeepot back on the heater, unable to keep her eye from the clock.

The diner closed at midnight. Every night at eleven fifty-five on the dot, he came in.

Tonight, though, eleven fifty-five came and went. And eleven fifty-six, eleven fifty-seven.

She'd have to close up. Bo, the owner, liked everything shut down right at midnight. He'd come in about fifteen minutes later and start going through the accounts for the day.

Eleven fifty-eight. The last customer, a farmer in a John Deere cap he must have picked up forty years ago, grinned at her and said, "Night, Addie. Time to go home to the wife."

He said that every night. Addie only nodded and gave him a warm good-bye.

Eleven fifty-nine. In one minute, she'd have to lock the door, turn the "Open" sign around to "Closed," help with the cleanup, and then go home. Her sister and two kids would be asleep, school day tomorrow. Addie would creep in as usual, take a soothing shower, play on the Internet a little to unwind, and then fall asleep. Her unwavering routine.

Tonight, though, she wouldn't be able to analyze every single thing the white-and-black-haired man said to her and decide whether he liked her or was just making conversation.

The second hand on the analog clock above the pass to the kitchen swept down from the twelve toward the six. Eleven-fifty nine and thirty seconds. Forty. Forty-five.

Addie sighed and moved to the glass front door.

Which opened as she approached it, bringing in the warmth of a Texas night, and the man.

Addie quickly changed reaching for the door's lock to yanking the door open wide and giving him her sunniest smile. "Hello, there. Y'all come on in. You made it just in time."

The big man gave her his polite nod and walked past her with an even stride, his black denim coat brushing jeans that hugged the most gorgeous ass Addie had seen in all her days. Because this diner's clientele had plenty of men from all walks of life, she'd seen her fair share of not-so-good backsides in jeans or showing inappropriately over waistbands.

Her man was different. His behind was worth a second, third, and fourth look. He was tall but not lanky, his build that of a linebacker in fine training, his shoulders and chest stretching his black T-shirt. The footwear under the blue jeans was always either gray cowboy boots or black motorcycle boots. Tonight, it was the motorcycle boots, supple leather hugging his ankles.

And, as always, Addie's man carried the sword. He kept it wrapped in dark cloth, a long bundle he held in his hand and tucked beside his seat when he sat down and ordered. At first Addie had thought the bundle held a gun—a rifle or shotgun—and she'd had to tell him that Bo didn't allow firearms of any kind in his diner. She'd lock it up for him while he ate. They had a special locker for the hunters who were regulars.

The man had shot her a quizzical look from his incredibly sexy eyes, pulled back the cloth, and revealed the hilt of a sword.

A sword, for crap's sake. A big one, with a silver hilt. Addie had swallowed hard and said that maybe it was okay if he kept it down beside his chair. He'd given her a curt nod and covered the hilt back up.

But that was just him. He was like no man Addie had ever met in her life. His eyes were an amazing shade of green she couldn't look away from. The eyes went with his hard face, which had been knocked around in his life, but he still managed to be handsome enough to turn the head of whatever woman happened to be in this late. Which, most nights, was only Addie.

His hair, though, was the weirdest thing. It was white, like a Scandinavian white blond, but striped with black. As though he'd gone in for a dye job one day and left it half finished. Or maybe he simply liked the look.

Except, Addie would swear it was natural. Dyes left an unusual sheen or looked brittle after a while. His hair glistened under the lights, each strand soft, in a short cut that suited his face. Addie often studied his head as he bent over his pie, and she'd clutch her apron to keep from reaching out and running her fingers through his interesting hair.

In sum—this man was hotter than a Texas wind on a dry summer day. Addie could feel the sultry heat when she was around him. At least, she sure started to sweat whenever she looked at him.

For the last month or so, he'd come in every night near to closing time, order the last pieces of banana cream pie and the apple pie with streusel, and eat while Addie locked the door and went through her rituals for the night. When Bo arrived through the back door, the man would go out the front, taking his sword ... and the other things he always brought.

They came in now, walking behind him—three little boys, the oldest one following the two younger ones. The oldest's name was Robbie, and he brought up the rear, looking around as though guarding his two little brothers.

"Hello, Robbie," Addie said. "Brett, Zane. How are you tonight?"

As usual, the two littlest chorused *Fine*, but Robbie only gave her a polite nod, mimicking his father. Although Addie thought the man wasn't actually Robbie's father.

The youngest ones had the man's green eyes and white-and-black hair, but Robbie didn't look like any of them. He had dark brown hair and eyes that were gray—a striking-looking kid, but Addie figured he wasn't related to the others. Adopted maybe, or maybe a very distant relative. Whatever, the man looked after all three with protective fierceness, not letting anyone near them.

They took the four stools at the very end of the counter away from the windows, almost in the hall to the bathrooms. Robbie sat on the seat farthest from the door, Zane and Brett perched in the next two seats with their dad next to them, his bulk between them and whoever might enter the diner.

Addie took up the coffeepot and poured a cup of fully caffeinated brew for black-and-white guy and three ice waters for the boys. She'd offered them cokes the first time they came into the diner but their dad didn't like them having sugared drinks.

Considering how much pie they put away, Addie didn't blame him. Sweet sodas on top of that would have them wired to the gills all night.

"You almost missed the pie," Addie said to the boys as she set dripping glasses of water in front of them. "We had a run on it today. But I saved you back a few pieces in the fridge." She winked. "I'll just run and get them. That's three banana creams and an apple streusel, right?"

She looked into the father's green eyes, and stopped.

She'd never seen him look at her like that. There was a hunger in his gaze—powerful, intense hunger. He skewered her with it. Addie looked back at him, her lips parting, her heart constricting.

Men had looked at her suggestively before but they'd always accompanied the look with a half-amused smile as though laughing at themselves, or telling Addie she'd have a great time if she conceded.

This was different. Black-and-white man studied her with a wanting that was palpable, as though any second he'd climb over the counter and come at her.

After a second, he blinked and the look was gone. He hadn't intended her to catch him.

The blink showed Addie something else. Behind the interest, his eyes held great distraction and deep worry.

Something had happened tonight, some reason he'd come here going on five minutes late.

Addie knew better than to ask if everything was all right. He wouldn't tell her. The man was not one for casual conversation. The boys talked but kept their answers general. They had never betrayed with one word where they were from, where they went to school, what they liked to do for fun, or why their dad kept them up this late every night.

Addie simply said, "I'll be right back," and ducked into the kitchen to fetch the pie.

She took out the pieces, already sliced on their plates, and sprinkled a little extra cocoa powder on the banana cream ones from the dented shaker on the shelf.

Jimmy, the guy who washed dishes, wasn't there. He liked to duck out for a smoke right at closing time, coming back in when Bo got there to finish the cleanup. Addie hummed, alone in the kitchen, her pulse still high from that look black-and-white man had given her.

If Addie marched out there and said to him, sure, she was interested — in a discreet way in front of his kids — would he break down and tell her his name?

Or would he take her somewhere and make love to her with silent strength, the same way he walked or ate his piece of pie, as though he savored every bite? Would Addie mind that?

She pictured him above her in the dark, his green eyes on her while she ran her hands all over his tight, beautiful body.

Nope, she wouldn't mind that at all.

She picked up two pieces of pie, still humming. At the same time, she heard a scratching at the back door.

Bo? Addie set down the pie and walked over. Bo always used his key to get in — they kept the back door locked. Even in the small town of Loneview that was pretty safe, robbers passing through might seize an opportunity.

Bo often couldn't get his key into the lock — his hands shook with a palsy that ran in his family. Jimmy often had to help him, or Addie would open the door for him. Bo was a bit early, but he was sometimes.

Addie reached for the door just as something banged into it.

"Bo? You okay?" Addie unlocked the deadbolt and carefully turned the doorknob.

The door fell inward, a heavy weight on it. Addie looked down.

A curious detachment came over her as she saw Jimmy the dishwasher, a guy of about thirty with greasy brown hair and beard stubble. He was dead, his brown eyes staring sightlessly. She knew he was dead because he had a gaping red hole where his heart used to be.

If this had been a movie, Addie would be screaming, fainting, sobbing, saying *Oh my God,* or running outside crying, *Somebody, help!*

Instead, she stood there, as though caught in treacle, unable to move, think, talk, or even breathe.

A faint noise sounded outside, and Addie raised her head. She saw the round muzzle of a gun, one of the automatic ones that shot however many rounds a minute. Her breath poured back into her lungs, burning, and she knew she was looking at her own death.

A rush of air passed her, and the door slammed shut. At the same time a pair of strong arms closed around her, propelling her to the floor, the man with black-and-white hair landing on top of her.

In the front of the diner, every window shattered as bullets flew through them. Glass exploded through the open pass between the kitchen and dining area, as did bullets, shards of cups and plates, tatters of napkins.

The kids, Addie thought in panic. *Where were the boys?*

There they were, huddled against the door to the freezer. How the man had gotten them in here so fast and out of sight Addie didn't know, but her body went limp with relief to see them.

"Who's doing this?" Addie squeaked. "What—"

The man clamped his hand over her mouth. "Shh." His voice was a low rumble. "I need to you to be very quiet, all right?"

End of Excerpt

About the Author

New York Times bestselling and award-winning author Jennifer Ashley has written more than 75 published novels and novellas in romance, urban fantasy, and mystery under the names Jennifer Ashley, Allyson James, and Ashley Gardner. Her books have been nominated for and won Romance Writers of America's RITA (given for the best romance novels and novellas of the year), several *RT BookReviews* Reviewers Choice awards (including Best Urban Fantasy, Best Historical Mystery, and Career Achievement in Historical Romance), and Prism awards for her paranormal romances. Jennifer's books have been translated into more than a dozen languages and have earned starred reviews in *Booklist*.

More about Jennifer's books and series can be found at www.jenniferashley.com

Printed in Great Britain
by Amazon